MIDDLE OF NOWHERE

Middle of Nowhere

Caroline Adderson

GROUNDWOOD BOOKS
HOUSE OF ANANSI PRESS
TORONTO BERKELEY

Groundwood Books / House of Anansi Press
110 Spadina Avenue, Suite 801, Toronto, Ontario M5V 2K4
or c/o Publishers Group West
1700 Fourth Street, Berkeley, CA 94710

We acknowledge for their financial support of our publishing program the
Canada Council for the Arts, the Government of Canada through the Canada
Book Fund (CBF) and the Ontario Arts Council.

Canada Council   Conseil des Arts   ONTARIO ARTS COUNCIL
for the Arts   du Canada   CONSEIL DES ARTS DE L'ONTARIO

Library and Archives Canada Cataloguing in Publication
Adderson, Caroline
Middle of nowhere / Caroline Adderson.
ISBN 978-1-55498-131-1 (bound).--ISBN 978-1-55498-132-8 (pbk.)
I. Title.
PS8551.D3267M53 2012   jC813'.54   C2011-906894-X

Cover illustration by Simon Ng
Design by Michael Solomon

Groundwood Books is committed to protecting our natural environment.
As part of our efforts, the interior of this book is printed on paper that contains
100% post-consumer recycled fibers, is acid-free and is processed chlorine-free.

Printed and bound in Canada

For Joan and Graham Sweeney

1

I HEARD A SIREN in my sleep. I thought it was Artie, but the sound came closer and got louder. Then, just outside our apartment building, it stopped. But not before it woke Artie, who picked up exactly where the siren left off.

"*Wa-wa-wa!*" Artie went.

A light swept through the room, then again, painting the walls red each time.

The police. Not exactly who I wanted to see. I stared at the lights, hoping they weren't for us, while Artie wailed on and on. He can be hard to stop.

Then I remembered the PNE and the giant beam that shines out of the fairground and circles the whole sky at night.

"Look at that light," I told Artie. "Do you remember the Exhibition last summer?"

He stopped wailing, just like the siren, and sat up staring at the red swirls.

"Is there a ferris wheel outside?"

"Let's look," I said.

We got out of bed and opened the curtains the rest of the way. It wasn't the police.

Artie climbed onto the back of the couch and perched there with his bare feet on the window-sill. He watched what was happening across the street like it was on TV.

"An ambulance! Look! They're coming out of that house!"

The old lady's house across the street. They were carrying her out on a stretcher, sliding her into the back of the ambulance, slamming the door.

Artie sang along as the ambulance drove away. *"Wa-wa-wa! Wa-wa-wa!"*

THE NEXT MORNING I looked out the window again. The drapes were closed in the house across the street, like it was asleep. It was a little house, one story and covered with stucco that had bits of broken glass mixed in. I felt sorry for it because there were apartments all around it now. It was the only house on the block that hadn't gone extinct. But I didn't really feel sorry for the old lady who lived there, who never said hi even though Artie and I walked past her house every single school day.

One Saturday, the old lady was out watering her garden. She was the only person in the neighborhood who grew flowers. We walked by with Mom and the lady made a sound like a grunt as we passed. I don't know what she was trying to say, but it didn't sound very nice.

Today was the last day I thought we could get away with the I-forgot-my-lunch excuse. On the way to school I told Artie to use it one more time.

"But I didn't forget my lunch," he said. "You didn't make me one."

"Tell her *I* forgot, then."

"You didn't, though. You're talking about it now."

Artie is five and a half and what you'd call "literal." He didn't understand that we were running out of food. If you forgot your lunch, Mrs. Gill would ask everybody in the class to contribute something. But if it happened too often, or more than twice in a row, she'd get suspicious and phone to find out if anything was wrong at home. I knew this for a fact because Artie's teacher, Mrs. Gill, was my kindergarten teacher, too, six years ago.

"Artie," I said as we walked past the house of the old lady they took away in the ambulance. "Let's pretend. Let's pretend I have amnesia."

"What's that?"

"It's when you get knocked on the head and you can't remember anything."

Suddenly he remembered the night before.

"Is that why the ambulance came?"

"Exactly! Except when the first-aid guys got to the door, I couldn't remember why I called them so I sent them away. Tell that to Mrs. Gill. Because of my amnesia I forgot to make your lunch again." I thought that sounded like the crazy sort of thing kindergarten teachers hear every day.

"Okay," Artie said.

"And don't mention Mom's away."

We had already discussed this. He nodded to show he understood how important it was that we kept this information to ourselves.

"And if you get a lot of stuff, don't eat it all," I said. "Bring some home."

AT THE END of the day I spread out on the table everything that Artie had brought from school. Cheese stick, fruit leather, four halves of different kinds of sandwiches — jam, ham and cheese, plain cheese, and something that looked like butter.

A butter sandwich? The kid probably ate the meat and just handed over the bread. A granola bar and an apple.

I took our last can of tomato soup from the cupboard and heated it with more water than the label said, so it would seem like more. Then the phone rang and I ran to answer it.

"Mom?" I said.

"I'm looking for Debbie," a man said.

"She's out."

"This is Greg, from Pay-N-Save."

Thump, thump, thump, thump, thump. I put my hand to my chest, but it was Artie in Mom's room throwing a ball against the wall.

"Greg," he said again. "Her boss? Maybe she forgot she had one. Can you give her a message?"

"Sure," I said, trying to sound casual. This time the *thump, thump, thump* really *was* my heart.

"Tell her not to bother coming back. Ever. She's blown it." Then he said, "I'm surprised. She was a good worker. Honest, dependable. Or so I thought — "

I hung up on him and went back to the kitchen counter, still thumping. I kept back one of the sandwich halves and the cheese stick for Artie's lunch the next day, even though I was one hundred per cent positive that Mom would turn up by morning. She'd go back to Pay-N-Save Gas and Greg would change his mind. Then, when we woke up, she would be home again, pouring out cereal for us.

I divided the rest of the food Artie brought home and splashed the soup into bowls. My hands were shaking.

"Supper's ready!"

AFTER SUPPER I made Artie take a bath. I had to wrestle him down to get his shirt off.

"I had a bath last night!" he said.

"You didn't."

"I did! I did!" he shrieked. The thing is, he really thought he had. He has no concept of time. When I finally got the shirt off and tossed it on the pile in the corner, an idea came to me.

"It's not actually a bath. It's laundry."

"I'm not laundry!"

All the light-colored things went in the tub with some bubble bath drizzled on top. As soon as the bubbles bubbled up and the clothes rose to the top, Artie whooped and stripped naked and jumped in.

"This is how they make wine," I told him as he sloshed around.

"From dirty clothes?"

I tricked him into sitting down and bouncing around for a bit until he and the laundry were clean. He seemed happy. But later, after I read him a story and tucked him in the hideaway bed, he started crying again.

"When's Mom coming back?"

"Soon."

"Where is she?"

"I don't know. But when she comes back, she'll be so happy our clothes are clean."

He pitched another fit. Artie's fits are straight out of horror movies. The little kid explodes and — surprise! There's a monster inside him.

"Something really good is going to come out of this, Artie," I promised.

He stopped bawling. "How do you know?"

"Because that's what happened last time she went away and came back," I said.

"Did she bring us a present?"

"She brought me a present."

"What was it?" he asked.

"You," I said.

Artie thought about this while he ground his fist into his eye. Then he exploded again.

"I miss her!"

"What do you miss?"

"I miss sucking her hair!"

Every night that she didn't have a class, Mom lay down with Artie and let him suck her hair until he fell asleep.

"Suck your own hair."

"It doesn't reach! And it's not the same! I miss how she smells!"

"How she smells? Why didn't you say?"

In the bathroom a giant bottle of Economizer Extra-Strength Hand and Body Lotion sat on the windowsill. I pumped some into my palm. Back in the living-room, I dried Artie's tears with the sheet, then I dabbed some of the lotion on his cheeks. At first he shoved my hand away, but as soon as he smelled the lotion he closed his eyes and let me rub his whole face with it.

"Mom?" he whispered. "Mom, I smell you. I smell you coming closer. I smell you coming home."

2

I was so sure that she would be back the next morning, but she wasn't. She didn't show up. She would, though. Soon. I was sure of it.

I was.

Mr. Bryant stopped me after class and said if I didn't bring back the permission form, I couldn't go on the field trip.

"We have a field trip?"

He took a lunging step forward and swung his arm like he was launching a bowling ball down the hall.

"Oh, right," I said.

"If it's the fee," he said, pretending to pick something off his sleeve so I wouldn't be embarrassed, "it doesn't matter."

Mr. Bryant is maybe my favorite teacher ever, though Mrs. Gill was pretty nice, too. Mr. Bryant calls us "people," but the best thing about him is that he wears earrings.

The first day of grade six this kid, Mickey Roach, put up his hand and asked Mr. Bryant if he was a lady. Mr. Bryant said he was a person, and he expected us all to act like people, too.

"What's that supposed to mean?" Mickey asked. Mr. Bryant explained that human beings bore a grave responsibility because we've evolved. It was our duty to demonstrate tolerance and compassion just as it was our duty to exercise the extraordinary reasoning abilities only human beings possess. He said we would be studying all about this in science, in social studies, in language arts, in every subject across the whole curriculum, because it was what really mattered. Then he congratulated Mickey for being the first one in the class to show an interest in the subject.

None of us really understood what he was on about, but I went home and asked if I could get my ears pierced anyway. Mom said no. She said I needed new shoes first.

In the hall, Mr. Bryant waited for my answer. I looked right at his gold pirate earrings and wondered, should I tell him?

I wanted to. But I couldn't because he would contact Social Services. As a teacher, it would be his duty.

"I hate bowling," I said.

So THAT WAS how I ended up at home on Friday morning. I took Artie to school and when I came back, I went straight to Mom's room and got her wallet out from under the cardboard box that she used as her bedside table. It was where she hid things ever since we were broken into. Burglars broke in, but they didn't take anything, not even the computer. It sounds weird, but that made me feel even worse. Like everything we owned was junk.

The day of the non-robbery, Mom came to me after Artie was asleep.

"I do own something valuable." She held out a tiny box.

"What's that?" I thought there would be a diamond ring or a gold nugget inside.

It was a tooth.

"Do you know who gave that to me?" she asked.

"Who?"

"Mrs. Pennypacker."

It was my tooth. I closed the box and handed it back to her. I didn't like to think about that time in foster care with the Pennypackers.

Mom was robbed at the gas station once, too, by a boy waving a steak knife. He took her wallet and all the money in the register, which is why she always left her wallet behind when she went to work and only took her bus fare and fifty cents for the phone. She would sit in the lit-up booth all night and study for her high-school-equivalency exam, which is for adults who never finished high school and want another chance. After she passed that, she wanted to become a nursing assistant or even a nurse.

I emptied Mom's wallet on the bed. Pictures of me and Artie, a bank card I didn't know the PIN for, a credit card, her community college ID. There was still a five-dollar bill and enough change to bring it almost to seven, and a huge wad of coupons. If I could have exchanged the coupons for money, we could have gone another month. Not that we'd have to, since I was positive Mom would show up in the next day or two.

Just as I was thinking that — that Mom would come home or at least call — the phone rang.

"Congratulations! You're the lucky winner of a Caribbean cruise! Press five to claim your prize. Press five now. Please press five."

I hung up and went out. Across the street, the little house was awake now. Somebody had opened the drapes.

One block up, on the corner of Broadway, was the Pit Stop Mart. The whole block smelled like old fried chicken grease from Chancey's Chicken down the street.

I bought four apples, a jug of milk and a dozen hotdog buns from the clerk with the gold front tooth. The hotdogs I had to put back in the cooler because there wasn't enough money. With the change, I got some penny candy to bribe Artie with if he pitched another fit that night and the lotion treatment didn't work.

I walked home, past the apartment blocks with their balconies crowded with plastic flower pots and plastic furniture and clothes racks draped in underwear. And mops. We lived on the ground floor with a sawed-down broom handle wedged in tight so the window couldn't be opened from the outside.

Then I saw the old lady. I saw the old lady and I froze where I was on the sidewalk and just stared at her. I guess I thought she was never coming back. The old lady, I mean. I was so sure Mom would be home first. I actually thought the old lady had died, but there she was, sitting on the bottom step of the last house left on the block wearing that little knitted cap with wisps of white hair sticking out, a man's shirt and those big glasses. There was something like a three-sided ladder made of shiny chrome standing in front of her. A walker.

And I felt sick when I saw her. Sick, because who was dead then? Who was dead?

"You!" she called. "Come over here, would you?"

I crossed the street and stopped in front of her closed gate. There was a sign on it that read ABSO-LUTELY NO FLYERS!

"You been to the store?" she asked.

I held up the plastic bag by the handles.

"I saw you. I waved to you from the window, but you hurried by so fast." She just sat there with her speckled hands on her knees, scowling at me through her glasses. "I don't normally ask for help."

She was stuck. She couldn't get up off the step.

I went through the ABSOLUTELY NO FLYERS! gate and offered my arm. The way she grabbed it and held on tight, I realized that she was scared of falling. If I hadn't come by, who knew how long she would have sat there? I really had to haul to get her up.

The second she was on her feet, she reached for the chrome walker and clutched it just as hard.

I waited until she was steady. "Okay?"

"I wanted you to go for me," she said, taking a twenty-dollar bill from her slacks pocket and put-ting it in my hand.

"To the store?" I said.

"Hold on." She switched hands that held the metal rail and took a list and a five-dollar bill from the other pocket. "This is what I need and that's for you. You're not going to run off with my money, are you?"

"No," I said. "Here." I put my bag down on the walk and left it with her as security. I felt dizzy with good luck, or maybe it was just that I hadn't eaten anything since supper the night before.

Back in the Pit Stop, I bought the hotdogs to go with the buns I'd already got. I bought the things on her list and made sure I kept the change separate from mine. The package of hotdogs I put in that big pocket on the side of my pants that I never used. They fit exactly.

When I got back, she was still there hanging onto the walker.

"Could you take it into the house? Put it on the kitchen table."

I did. I went up the steps and inside. The kitchen was straight ahead. When I came back out she asked if I'd take her in, too, which I did.

"Don't forget the thingie," she said, waving to it.

She kept one freckled hand on the stair railing, the other on my arm. Inside the door, I set the walker down, making sure she was gripping it before I let her go.

I tried to give her change back. I really did.

⌒

As soon as I got in our apartment, I dropped the groceries on the floor and went over to the wall and stood on my head. Once, in art class, Mr. Bryant showed us how copying a drawing upside down makes it come out better. You look at it in a different way, I guess. So I stood on my head and looked differently at that awful question.

Who was dead?

Now everything in the room was upside down. What a mess. Did I need to be upside down to notice the hideaway bed was not hiding and not made? That dirty breakfast dishes were still on the table and damp laundry draped all over the chairs? It was a one-bedroom apartment. Mom got the bedroom because she slept during the day. Artie and I shared the hideaway bed. We didn't dare leave the bed open with Mom around. Artie would never bounce a ball against the wall if she was there.

If somebody ever suspected Artie and I were on our own, they would come straight over and the mess would give us away. Obviously, there wasn't a mother for miles around here.

The blood drained from my feet and the hot-dogs slid out of my pocket and bounced on the carpet. I stayed upside down for as long as I could. Then I kicked off the wall and landed on the floor in a ball. When I tried to sit up again, I toppled right over on my side.

That was probably how the old lady felt. Dizzy. Dizzy and scared. But after a minute, I got up fine on my own.

I never did see an answer to my question.

UNTIL IT WAS time to get Artie, I spent the rest of Friday cleaning the apartment. The vacuum cleaner was broken so I had to pick the dirt off the carpet, go around collecting little bits of stuff with my fingers. I did a good job because as soon as we got in, Artie went running to Mom's bed-room, calling, "You're back! You're back!"

Then he pitched another one.

Economizer Extra-Strength Hand and Body Lotion — it's great for fits!

They should put that on the label.

ARTIE'S AFRAID OF lots of things. The old lady across the street. Dogs. Men with beards. But his most annoying fear is of falling in the toilet.

Last year, when he was four and a half, he woke up in the middle of the night and went to the bathroom half asleep. He didn't notice the seat was up. Screams! Mom and I went running and there he was, arms and legs waving in the air.

"Help! I'm going down! I'm going down!" Ever since, there's no convincing him that he's way too big to be flushed away. And even now he needs somebody to hold his hand if he has to sit down.

Those were the times I really, really wished Mom was back. Saturday morning, Sunday morning, standing there holding his hand and gagging and wishing he would hurry up.

Still, we survived the whole weekend on the old lady's five dollars and the change from the twenty she gave me. Hotdogs for breakfast, hotdogs for lunch, hotdogs for supper. On Sunday morning I went back to the Pit Stop Mart and spent the rest on cereal for a little variety in our diet.

I took a shower and when I came out, Artie was rolling around on the floor with the phone tucked under his chin, chattering away, the way he did when Mom called from her class to say goodnight.

I snatched it from him.

"Mom?"

"On a scale of one to ten, ten being the most likely — " the woman on the other end of the line was saying, " — how likely would you be to choose a sugar-free soft drink over a regular soft drink, regardless of the brand?"

ON A SCALE of one to ten, ten being the most likely, I would have ranked Mom being there when we got home from school on Monday as a ten. Maybe a nine, but no lower than that. She'd been gone a week.

We always wake her when we get home from school. Her shift at Pay-N-Save started at eleven at night, so she had to leave the apartment by ten to catch the bus, unless she had a class. If she had a class, she left after supper and went to work from school. She got home in the morning in time to eat breakfast with us and make our lunches and see us off. After school, Artie would come and lie on top of her and bury his nose in her neck. When that didn't work, he'd steal her earplugs and lift the satiny edge of her eye mask and growl.

Anyway, she wasn't there so I poured out some dry cereal for Artie and put him in front of the TV. Then I sat in the window and watched the house across the street. I hadn't seen the old lady all weekend, but the drapes had opened and closed and the lights went on at night and the TV colored her living-room blue. She would run out of food sooner or later, just like us. Or maybe she had somebody she could call — grown-up kids or grandkids.

Then I thought of something else. It was right in front of my eyes, but for some reason I didn't see it until that moment.

The next morning on the way to school, I took Artie across the street to look at the old lady's garden. Before her ambulance ride, she used to be out there all the time, watering her plants and not saying hi to us. I didn't know anything about plants, but they looked thirsty to me. I was going to offer to do the watering for her because I hoped she might pay me.

Artie pulled on my hand.

"Come on, Curtis. She's in the window."

That was what I wanted. I pretended not to see her or notice when she stepped away from the window.

"Let's go!"

I needed to give her enough time to hobble to the door. It took forever. She moved so slowly with that thing. Finally she bashed her way out onto the step, holding the screen with one hand, clutching the walker with the other, scowling at us from under the knitted cap. Artie nearly fainted on the spot.

"Do you need any help?" I called.

"Do *you*?" she called back.

I thought she meant that she'd been watching our place at the same time I'd been watching hers. That she'd noticed a twelve-year-old going out with his five-and-a-half-year-old brother. That an adult never came out with them. Not once for a whole week.

I grabbed Artie and we took off.

It wasn't a good day after that. At school I found it hard to concentrate. Mr. Bryant asked me if everything was okay and I told him yes. But at that exact moment my stomach let rip the loudest gurgle you ever heard. It sounded like a flushing toilet. Mr. Bryant dropped his eyes to where the sound came from, as though I had a wild animal stuffed under my shirt. Or maybe he was looking at my shirt, which was one of the ones Artie had washed in the bathtub. It didn't look too clean, even though he'd stomped all over it.

Great, I thought. Now *two* people are suspicious.

Maybe Mrs. Gill was, too, because instead of a lunch, I'd packed Artie the penny candy I'd bought on Friday.

But I wasn't out of ideas yet. I had a few and one was bottles, so after school Artie and I went down to the creepy underground parking garage and checked the recycling.

It turned out I wasn't the only one to think of this. Margarine tubs and dirty ravioli cans spilled out of the bin, but they weren't anything we could cash in at the store. The beer cans and liquor bottles had already been scooped up.

So after the last Mr. Noodle split between us, I got the credit card from mom's wallet under the cardboard box in her bedroom. While Artie drew a picture, I practiced copying *Debbie Schlanka* over and over off the back of the card. She had a pretty easy-to-forge signature. It didn't look that different from how I wrote Curtis Schlanka. I realized this was because she never got that far in school. She only made it to grade nine before she quit.

My son Curtis Schlanka has permission to use this card. Best wishes.

I held it up. The "best wishes" looked dumb. It wasn't a birthday card! I wrote it again without any closing.

Using a credit card with a forged permission note was pretty much the same as stealing. If we were caught, the Pit Stop Mart clerk would call the police. Then Social Services would get involved. Most foster families only take in one kid at a time. They have their own kids like Mrs. and Mr. Pennypacker had Brandon. I could look after myself, but what about Artie?

The clerk with the gold front tooth was working at the Pit Stop again. He lifted his face out of a magazine as we came in and watched me take a basket. My heart started thumping.

Artie made straight for the candy.

"No," I said, dragging him to the cooler at the back where the milk was. I wanted to fill the basket with food, but thought it would look suspicious if we bought too many groceries at the Pit Stop Mart, even though it was where I'd been buying everything because the supermarket was a bus ride away. I put in milk, apples, carrots, bread, sandwich meat, cheese spread, cans of fruit, packages of soup.

Artie didn't want carrots. He wanted a Slushie.

"No Slushie," I said.

"I want candy. I want candy for lunch like you gave me today."

"Shh. You were supposed to trade it for some real food. Remember? Did you?"

He crinkled his nose.

"Well, you can't have more candy. You'll get sick. You'll get rickets."

"What's rickets?"

"It's a disease. Your legs bow out and get so weak you can't walk. You get it from eating too much candy."

I shushed him again as we got close to the counter. Somebody else had come in and was buying cigarettes and lottery tickets. On his way out, he tossed the cigarette wrapper on the floor. The clerk glared after him, then kept on glaring as I heaved our basket onto the counter. He started scanning our stuff as though *we* had thrown the wrapper down. I took the credit card from my pocket. The note was folded around it and my fingers stuck to the paper as I handed it to him.

He looked at it with one eyebrow lifted. Then he looked at me the same way and my face got hot. I thought we were goners except just then, Artie reached up with the cigarette wrapper and put it on the counter where it unballed in slow motion.

"He littered," Artie said.

And the clerk smiled. He showed his gold tooth to us, then snatched up the wrapper and tossed it in the garbage.

"Anything else? Scratch and win?" he asked, all friendly now.

"Okay," I said.

He swiped the credit card and handed me a pen to sign the receipt.

"Should I sign my name or my mom's name?" I asked.

"Your name." He passed the groceries over the counter in two bulging bags. "Good luck."

I think he meant the lottery ticket. We scratched it outside the store, and even though we didn't win anything, I still felt lucky.

BEFORE BED WE treated ourselves to bread and canned peaches, the bread dipped in the syrup and all soppy with it. It should have been easy to get to sleep because my stomach was finally full. Mom hadn't come back yet or even called but I was still ten out of ten positive she would be back. Because that was what she promised a long time ago when I was living with the Pennypackers.

That she would never leave me again.

Also, our problems were solved. Our one problem, really. All I had to do was wave the credit card and the door of the Pit Stop Mart would swing open. Food was as good as free now.

I was too excited to sleep. While Artie snored beside me, I lay thinking of everything else we could buy. Things like clothes or a new toy for Artie. Or a skateboard, not for Artie. I wondered why Mom was always saying we couldn't afford things when we had this magic card.

But the next morning, the excited feeling was gone. I woke up remembering back when I was in kindergarten, waiting for Mom to pick me up. That day Mrs. Gill gave me an alphabet puzzle to do. Mom still hadn't come by the time I finished it, so Mrs. Gill asked if I wanted to help her.

Did I? I loved helping but hardly ever got the chance. Everybody wanted to be her helper. Now I was the only one there and I hoped so hard that Mom wouldn't show up before I finished helping.

My job was to go around the room with a bag of cotton balls. I felt very important taking out a fistful of the soft balls and leaving them on each table.

"We're going to make Santas for Christmas," Mrs. Gill told me.

Mom didn't show up and I was glad except that there was nothing else to do after that. Mrs. Gill was writing something in her lesson book so I went over and climbed in her lap. She put the pencil down. It was raining and water was dribbling down the windowpanes. We sat together, watching the drips make patterns on the glass.

After a few minutes she said, "Curtis, I think we'd better call her."

We phoned from the office. Mom didn't answer. I had the key around my neck in case of emergency and I showed it to Mrs. Gill. She said she would drive me home and wait with me until my mom came back. We lived in a different apartment then and it was a much longer walk to school so I was happy to drive in a car, especially in the rain.

On the way Mrs. Gill asked me questions. Had my mother ever forgotten me like this before? No. Was there somebody else who was supposed to pick me up? I said Gerry sometimes did. Who was Gerry? He was my mom's friend. Was he my father? No.

At the apartment, I unlocked the door and we went inside. Mrs. Gill put on her sad face. That was a game we played at circle time. She would put on a huge fake smile and ask, "What face is this?"

"Your happy face!" we would call. Sad face. Mad face. Thinking face. "I don't see any thinking faces," she would say when we weren't paying attention.

The sad face was about the bottles on the table.

While we waited, Mrs. Gill sat with me on the couch and took a book out of her purse.

"I always carry a book with me, Curtis. Just in case." It was about a frog who rode a motorcycle. After she finished reading it to me, she checked her watch and asked if I was hungry. In her purse was a granola bar.

"Also just in case," she said, putting on her happy face. Then she left me looking at the pictures of the motorcycling frog while she stepped into the hall to make some calls.

I tucked the granola bar down the back of the couch. Just in case there wasn't any supper that night.

I knew why Mom wasn't coming home. She wasn't coming home because I had hoped so hard that she wouldn't while I was helping Mrs. Gill with the cotton balls for Santa. But now I did want her home.

Mrs. Gill came back in. Did I know anybody in the building? No. Did I have relatives in town? No. Who was this Gerry person who was listed in the office as my emergency contact? Where did he live?

"Here," I said and got up and led her to the bedroom to show her Gerry's stuff. His clothes lying all over the floor — his jeans and dirty socks and the T-shirts with the sleeves ripped off. Gerry's guitar in the stickered case in the corner.

But everything was gone.

Gerry had left, I found out later. He'd left and Mom had gone after him.

3

CAN YOU GO TO THE STORE FOR ME?

It was taped to the front window, written in big letters so I could read it from the street. I went through the gate with the ABSOLUTELY NO FLYERS! sign and up the steps to ring the doorbell. Artie waited at the bottom, his knees practically knocking together in fear.

I wasn't afraid of her anymore. We had the credit card.

"I'm coming!" I heard her call from inside. "Don't run off on me again!"

Finally she opened the door, pink and cranky, before she remembered to put on her happy face.

Her teeth were brown. Maybe that was why she looked so sour all the time, because she was hiding her bad teeth.

"You saw my sign?" she asked, and I nodded. "Why'd you run off so fast yesterday?"

"You seemed mad."

"I *was* mad! You would be, too, if you had to pick up and set down this contraption every time you took a step!" Then she noticed Artie hovering at the bottom of the steps. Her face went soft like ice cream.

"Hello!" she called. "What's your name?"

Artie drew his lips into his mouth, making a tight line.

"Artie," I answered for him.

"Artie? I'm Mrs. Burt."

She didn't ask my name. She said, "Boys, it's a catastrophe. I'm out of tea."

We were on our way to school. She said she would probably survive if we brought the tea after school, being as she had already gone without for nearly twenty-four hours. "You may as well pick up a few other things at the same time. Milk and eggs. And cottage cheese. Should I write it down?"

"I'll remember," I said.

"You're sharp." She gave me another twenty-dollar bill. "And if there's anything left, get a treat for Artie and yourself."

"We don't need it."

"I'm sure you don't, but take it anyway."

THE REST OF the day went much faster. I had a sandwich in my stomach, as well as toast and milk from breakfast. Also the school year was winding down and not even the teachers were that serious anymore. It felt like one big art project now.

I picked up Artie at three and even stopped to chat with Mrs. Gill for a few minutes in case she wondered about his candy lunch the day before. She asked me how Mom was and I told her in a completely normal voice that she was great.

We bought the old lady's groceries. The same clerk was there and he flashed his gold tooth at us.

Suddenly I was grateful to her, to Mrs. Burt. It looked less suspicious if we sometimes bought things with cash. There was enough money left over so I got us a Slushie. A blue Slushie that we shared through two straws in the one hole in the lid while we sat on the steps of the Pit Stop Mart and breathed the fried-chicken air, watching the cars go by on Broadway and the homeless people rattle past with their carts.

Then we went to Mrs. Burt's place and rang her bell. Again, about a week went by before she got to the door. First, the TV shut off. After a few minutes, the walker knocked against something and she started muttering, "Blast it, blast it, blast it." Artie tensed up and squeezed my hand until she finally opened up.

A smell poured out over us, the most delicious smell. We both leaned into it.

"What happened? You two been drinking ink?" I looked at Artie and saw the Slushie had dyed his lips and tongue blue, and probably mine, too.

She motioned to the bag in my hand.

"Put it on the table."

I went ahead to the kitchen. Artie followed, still nervous, but drawn in by the smell. Mrs. Burt was much slower. When she finally caught up, Artie and I were standing there drooling at the cookies on the table, lined up on baking sheets in perfect even rows, like checkers.

I still had the grocery bag in one hand. She took it from me and said, "Go ahead. Help yourself."

Artie snatched two and crammed them in his mouth. I hoped my manners were better, but the cookies were still warm and so good. Meanwhile, Mrs. Burt went over to the fridge with the heavy bag and started to unload it, hanging the plastic handles on the walker, propping the door open with an elbow.

"Here," I said. "I'll do it."

She let me. The last thing in the bag was the box of tea.

"Halleluiah," she said when I handed it to her. Then she offered us milk, which I poured into glasses and brought to the table.

"Go ahead, Artie. Have as many as you want," she said, even though he'd already eaten about fifty. "Sit, sit down."

While she waited for the kettle, Mrs. Burt stood at the counter watching us. Well, she watched Artie. She didn't seem cranky now. More like somebody's cookie-making grandma.

"Artie with the legendary name," she said.

"What?" Artie asked, spraying crumbs.

"You know. King Arthur and all them."

"No."

"No?" She shook her head.

The sugar from the Slushie and all the cookies kicked in. Artie slithered off the seat of his chair and onto the floor.

"Artie," I said, warning him.

Mrs. Burt took the chair next to him and, plunking down her mug of tea, smiled at him down by her feet. He pinged the walker with his fingernail.

"Here, try this," she said, handing down her teaspoon. Different notes sounded on different rails and they both laughed. Then Mrs. Burt took a big slurp of tea and sighed.

"Do you have rickets?" Artie asked from the floor.

"Rickets? Certainly not."

"Then why do you have this thing?" He used it now, hand over hand, to get up off the floor.

"I fell down and almost busted a hip."

"Where'd you get it?"

"From the hospital."

"The ambulance took you away."

"It did."

"I like it," Artie said, giving the walker a pat. "You could dry clothes on it. We washed our clothes in the bathtub and hung them on the chairs. Then we had nowhere to sit."

"Don't you have a laundry room over there?" she asked.

"It costs a lot of quarters," Artie said.

I got worried then that he would give away even more personal information, so I stood up.

"Thanks very much, Mrs. — "

The phone rang. Mrs. Burt set her mug down hard and cut me off.

"Oh, shut up!"

And Artie scooted behind me in fright.

"Not *you*," Mrs. Burt told him. "Those tele-whatsits. Or if it's not them, it's Miss Big Shot in Toronto. It's just about killing me, running to the phone!"

It kept ringing, but she didn't get up.

"We have to go," I said. Mrs. Burt looked surprised, then hurt.

"Take some cookies," she said. "Put them on a plate." She looked right at me. "What's your name again?"

"Curtis," I told her for the first time.

Whoever was calling gave up then.

"Get a plate and load them on, Curtis," she said, rising and getting a head start, picking up and putting down her contraption all the way down the hall so she could get to the door first and be waiting with the five-dollar bill.

"It's fine," I said. "You don't have to pay me."

She snorted. "Unlike most people around here, I have pride."

I didn't know what she meant, but I knew it would insult her if I didn't take the money, so I took it.

"Is your mother at work?"

"Yes."

She pulled a pad from the pocket of her man's shirt. It had a little stub of pencil stuck in the coil binding.

"Here. Write your phone number down. I want to talk to her."

"What about?"

"I want to ask her if it's okay if you help me out until I don't need this thingie anymore. Do you want to? You can bring the legendary Artie."

"You don't have to call her. It's fine."

"I want to talk to her. I want her to know I'm not a charity case."

"She'll say it's fine."

"She can say it to me then."

I thought about writing the wrong phone number but that seemed pointless.

"When does she get home?" she asked.

"That's the thing," I said. "She works at night and sleeps in the day. Also, she's studying for exams."

"Exams? What kind of exams?"

"She's doing her high-school equivalency."

"Oh, a dropout." She sniffed. "Now bring that plate back tomorrow. Ring the doorbell. Don't just leave it on the steps or somebody'll steal it."

We thanked her. Then we crossed the street to our building where there wasn't a single flower growing out front. Just some prickly knee-high bushes decorated with wrappers and lids from take-out cups. Mrs. Burt was still standing in her doorway. Artie looked back and waved to her.

"She's not mean anymore," he said.

"Really?" I said.

I'd learned a lot this year in Mr. Bryant's class. Not just math and socials and health. All year Mr. Bryant set a high standard of behavior. We had to treat each other with respect. Respect meant we had to pay attention not only to *what* we said, but *how*. The how was almost more important. For example, I could say I thought you were smart, or nice, but if I said it a certain way, it would mean the opposite. At the beginning of the year I didn't notice the *how* because everybody talked to each other that way all the time. But now I noticed.

Like *how* Mrs. Burt said "dropout." Like it was the worst thing in the world.

In the lobby we stopped for the mail. I'd been taking it in but not opening it, just leaving it in a heap on the counter for Mom to deal with when she came back. If any of it had looked like a letter from Mom or to her I would have opened it, but it was mostly just bills and flyers.

Back in the apartment, the phone was already ringing. Mrs. Burt, I thought.

But it wasn't.

"Is Debbie there?" a man asked.

I knew it wasn't Greg from Pay-N-Save because the voice was different.

"No. Can I take a message?"

"When's she going to be in?"

"I'm not sure."

"Tell her to call Nelson about the rent. It came back NSF."

"What does that mean?" I asked.

"She'll know what I'm talking about. Tell her to put a new check in my box in the lobby. Not in the mail."

"Okay."

"She should call me to let me know it's there. I don't want to drive all the way across town and there's no check. Also she's got to add fifteen bucks on for the service charge."

"Okay," I said and hung up.

I opened the mail. The good news was there was a check from the government. Two hundred and eight dollars and fifty-six cents for the Child Tax Benefit payment, whatever that was.

Later that night I heard a siren. I thought of the ambulance that had taken Mrs. Burt away. Was it coming back?

No. The siren was in my head. It was screaming, *Rent! Rent! Rent!*

I got out of bed and wrote another note.

My son Curtis Schlanka has permission to cash this check.

UP ON BROADWAY, about half a block down from the Pit Stop Mart, next to Chancey's Chicken, was Dominion Check Cashing. I thought it would be safer than the bank which, last time we were in it with Mom, was full of nice people asking, "What can I do for you today, Ms. Schlanka?" and, "How old's your little boy, Ms. Schlanka?" and, "You have a great day, Ms. Schlanka."

In other words, they would wonder where our mom was.

The man in Dominion Check Cashing with the toothpick in the corner of his mouth and greasy hairs glued on his bald head looked at the check and said Mom had to come in herself.

"She's at work," I said.

The toothpick shifted to the other side of his mouth. "She can come after work."

"She finishes at, like, six in the morning."

He pointed to the neon sign in the window. I read OPEN 24 HOURS, backwards.

"What about the note?"

He nudged it back across the counter at me.

"Looks to me like you wrote that yourself. Are you stealing from your own mother?"

"No!" I said.

"Kids today. Ba-a-ad," he said, crossing his arms and settling back on his stool.

"I'm not bad!" Artie cried.

"Not yet," the man said, spitting out slivers. "But just you wait."

We stormed out. I wanted to slam the door, but it was glass with hinges that eased it closed. I marched ahead. Artie trotted behind me, saying loudly, "I'm good!"

A man in a dirty coat came along pushing a cart. He stopped and said in a gravelly voice, "Just how good are you, kid?"

"Really good!" Artie said. He didn't even notice the man had a beard. That's how mad he was.

"Show us. Sing a song or something."

"I'm a little teapot short and stout . . ." Artie began. He added the actions — one hand on his waist, the other stuck straight out while he tipped over and poured some imaginary tea onto the sidewalk.

Somebody with tattoos was coming out of the Pit Stop Mart, and he stopped to watch. A woman in the coin laundry smiled through the window. When Artie finished singing, everybody clapped. He took a bow.

"You *are* good," the man with the cart said. He lifted the plastic sheet off his stuff and started rooting around. "Here. This is for you. It's the Bird of Happiness."

It was a plastic bird with feathers glued all over it and wires sticking out of its feet. Some of the feathers had fallen off so it looked diseased. The woman from the laundromat came out and gave Artie the change she didn't need for the dryer and the tattooed man offered everybody gum. All because my funny little brother sang a kindergarten song.

That's the thing about Artie. He *is* good. He's the good thing that came out of a bad thing.

When I remembered that, I felt better.

If worst came to worst, I figured I could get him to sing and dance while I passed around a hat.

4

AFTER SCHOOL THE next day Mrs. Gill said she needed to speak with me. First I had to wait while she walked up and down the squirming line of kids, checking that they all had their shoes on the correct feet and their backpacks zipped and their own paper-plate ladybugs, not someone else's.

I remembered being in that line. When your mother showed up, or your brother, or whoever was assigned to pick you up, Mrs. Gill sang out your name and you got to fly away.

Today Artie was the last one and he looked pretty cross as Mrs. Gill waved me into the room. He had his grumpy face on.

"How are you, Curtis?

"Fine."

"How's everything at home?"

"Great."

"Artie?" Mrs. Gill said. "You may have Happy back now."

Artie pulled his bottom lip up to its normal place and dashed over to Mrs. Gill's desk. The Bird of Happiness was in the top drawer. Artie grabbed it and rubbed it all over his face.

"Poor Happy," he told it. "Were you scared in that dark drawer all alone?"

"Bring Happy here please, Artie," said Mrs. Gill in that firm, kind, kindergarten-teacher voice that is impossible to disobey. When Artie brought the bird over, Mrs. Gill said, "I won't take him from you again, Artie, but you must let Curtis see what I'm talking about." Mrs. Gill pointed to the wires in the hideous plastic feet. "Curtis," she said, "someone got poked today."

"By accident!" Artie wailed.

"By accident, but it still hurt. Poor Thompson. These are sharp wires. We can't have things with sharp wires in the classroom, Artie."

"He'll leave it at home," I said.

"I can't," Artie said. "I need Happy. If I don't have Happy, I'm sad."

"You only got Happy yesterday," I said. "You weren't sad before you got him."

"I was so! I miss Mom!" And he started to bawl.

Mrs. Gill reached for him and pulled him close.

"Curtis?" she asked. "Is your mother away?"

Just yesterday I had been thinking how special Artie was, how funny and adorable when he sang "I'm a Little Teapot" outside the laundromat. Now I wanted to grab that ugly, bald bird and stuff it down his throat.

I remembered Mrs. Burt saying, "Oh, shut up!" I wanted to say it now. *Oh, shut up, Artie!*

Shut up! Shut up! Shut up!

But I didn't, or Mrs. Gill would know for sure that I was lying when I told her, "She'll be gone for two days. Our neighbor's looking after us."

Before Mrs. Gill could ask Artie if this was true, he stopped kissing Happy and said, "Mrs. Burt?"

"Yes," I said. "Mrs. Burt's looking after us tonight. Tonight and tomorrow night. Then Mom will be back."

"She'll be back tomorrow night?"

"The day after that," I said, and Artie smiled and wiped his tears away.

We left school and headed for the store. Artie wanted Happy to sit on his shoulder. I explained that for Happy to sit on his shoulder, I would have to poke the wires through his shirt. Then he'd have holes in his shirt.

"Small holes."

"All right," I said. I was trying not to let him see how mad I was, but my hands were shaking, I was so mad. I just wanted to get to the Pit Stop Mart and buy some food, but now I had to stop and wire the plastic bird onto Artie's shoulder.

When I finished, it flopped right over.

Artie stood him up. "Ow," he said. "The wires poked me!"

"Now you know how that other kid felt."

I walked on so Artie had no choice but to trot after me. He held Happy upright, then let him go. Flop! He did it again. Flop!

"He won't sit up," Artie complained.

"He's sleeping," I said, though I really wanted to say that Happy was dead.

"Oh," Artie said. "Then *shhh*."

I was happy not to say anything. Until we reached the Pit Stop Mart, we didn't speak.

There was a different clerk this time who was talking on the phone in another language. She barely looked at us as we moved down the aisle, filling the basket.

"Happy wants a Slushie," Artie said.

"Too bad," I said. This made Artie suck in his lips. He trudged along behind me with the bird flopped over on his shoulder.

"What do birds eat?" he asked after a minute.

"Seeds," I said, though I should have said bread. It was already in the basket.

"Happy wants seeds."

"No seeds," I said.

I should have just bought a package of sunflower seeds. They were cheap and good for you, but I knew what would happen. It would be too hard for Artie to shell them. I would have to sit there for a week doing it for him, all so the dead, bald bird wired to his shoulder could pretend to eat. Then I would get fed up and Artie would snatch the package and spill them all over the carpet. It would be me, not him, on my hands and knees picking them up one by one.

"You have a grumpy face," Artie said.

I swung around and in a low, hissing voice said, "Do you remember what I told you about that kid Brandon Pennypacker? How he spat in my food? How he shrank my side of the room? Do you want to go and live with Brandon? Because that's what's going to happen if you go around telling people that Mom's away. They are going to send you to live with Mrs. Pennypacker and you won't have Mom and you won't have me. You'll have *Brandon*."

Artie's eyes rolled back in his head and his face went all purple. He shrieked and flung himself down and pounded the floor of Pit Stop Mart with his hands and feet.

The clerk was still talking on the phone. I knelt and apologized to Artie. I asked him to stop crying. When I tried to cover his mouth, the monster inside him bit me, so I left him there screaming and ran up the aisle where I'd seen toothbrushes and deodorant. I grabbed a bottle of baby lotion and dumped some in my hand. Then I ran back to Artie and smeared his face with it. He stopped screaming right away and sat up spitting.

The clerk bent over us on the floor. "What's going on?"

"Nothing," I said. "Sorry."

"Did you open that?" She pointed to the bottle in my hand. "You have to buy it now."

"I want to buy it." I put it in my basket. It cost $5.99 for a tiny, tiny bottle.

We got up off the floor and followed the clerk back to the counter, Artie rubbing his face, trying to get the lotion off.

"That doesn't smell like Mom! Not at all!"

I was too shocked by the awful thing I'd said to Artie to remember to feel nervous about the credit card. I passed it over, the note folded around it like before, but she didn't even read it. She just swiped the card and handed me a pen.

Now it almost seemed funny — me slathering Artie, him screaming. I glanced at him working his tongue in his mouth to get rid of the taste of the lotion. The bird was flopped backward over his shoulder. I laughed and he laughed.

The machine spat out the receipt. "Declined," the clerk said.

"What?"

"Declined."

"What does that mean?" I asked.

"It means the card's no good."

"I used it a couple of days ago."

"Well, you can't use it anymore. It's probably maxed out."

"What does that mean?"

She turned the card over and read the name. "That's your mom? She's over her limit. Go home and ask her if she's got another card."

"Okay," I said, stunned.

"I'll just put this behind the counter till you get back." She lifted the basket down.

"She's at work."

"Okay. Do me a favor then and put the milk back."

I returned the milk to the cooler and she didn't mention the lotion I was supposed to pay for.

As soon as we were out of the store I sat down

on the steps of the Pit Stop Mart and pitched a fit of my own. I put my face in my hands and cried for the first time since Mom left.

Artie just stood there. After a minute he started stroking my hair and when that didn't work, he ripped Happy off his shoulder and made him hop all over my head and tweet. The wires stabbed my scalp and hurt like hell, but I was glad. It made me cry harder.

Finally Artie gave up and started bawling, too. I figured we'd better do our crying at home or somebody would call the police.

Mrs. Burt was standing in her yard, her body squeezed between the walker's chrome rails. She had the hose out and, when she saw us, she started waving it in the air so the water sprayed all around her, catching the light.

"You-hoo! Fellas!"

And then we saw it — a rainbow, shimmering above her.

"You still got my plate!" she called.

And Artie pulled away from me and went running to her, full tilt.

"WHERE DO YOU think she's got to?" Mrs. Burt asked.

"I don't know," I said.

"Has she ever done something like this before?"

I didn't answer.

"I see," said Mrs. Burt.

We were sitting at her kitchen table, Artie drawing a picture of Mrs. Burt. I knew it was her because he'd drawn the walker, making it look like a ladder. In her hand was the hose with a rainbow shooting out of it.

After a big gulp of tea, Mrs. Burt patted her knitted cap and said, "I hate to tell you this, Curtis, but if she's done it before, she'll do it again."

"She won't," I said.

"People never change."

"They do," I said.

"I change," Artie said. "I change when my clothes are dirty. I wash them in the tub!"

"I've got a washing machine," Mrs. Burt offered. Then she asked, "Don't you have relatives?"

I told her my grandma died when my mom was in grade nine. All we really needed was to figure out the bills and the rent. I asked Mrs. Burt if she could help with that and she sent me home to get the stuff.

In the apartment I collected everything I could find, including the government check.

While I was there the phone rang. I froze,

staring at it. If I answered, it would be Nelson, the landlord, demanding the rent. If I didn't, it would be Mom. Mom calling to say where she was and what had happened and when she was coming back.

"Hello?" I said.

"Bring over some crayons or something so he can color his picture," Mrs. Burt said.

I DIDN'T REALLY understand how credit cards worked. There was this thing called interest. If you didn't pay back the credit card company every month, they added interest to your bill. The longer it took to pay, the more you had to pay, so the people with the least money ended up paying the most.

"That's why I never touch the things," Mrs. Burt said. "I'm not going to be cheated by anybody." She looked at the Child Tax Benefit check. "We could probably get this cashed."

"How?" I asked.

"Some poor little old lady could bring it in." And she smiled, showing her tea-colored teeth. "Then you can use it to pay the phone and the electricity. Or you can let the phone go and just use mine."

"What if Mom tries to call?"

Mrs. Burt looked at the ceiling and sighed. "You're right, though. If the phone's disconnected, people get suspicious. You should pay it."

"What about the rent? I don't even know how much it is."

"Ask him when he calls again. Say she lost his number. That's why she didn't leave out the check."

"But I don't have a check to leave out."

"Don't you have her checkbook?"

"I never looked."

"Well, look and leave out the check. It'll take a while to bounce. That'll buy you some time." With both hands on the walker, she hoisted herself up with a grunt. "Let's eat. Are you boys hungry?"

Ha ha ha.

I cleared the papers away and set the table. Then she asked me to put Artie's drawing on the fridge and carry the pot of chicken soup over to the table. The soup was delicious. Even Happy, who drank a few sips out of Artie's spoon, said it was.

Mrs. Burt said, "It's homemade. You probably never had homemade soup before. If there's any left," — I was filling my bowl for the third time — "you can take it home. It'll taste even better tomorrow."

After supper, Artie and I cleaned up while Mrs. Burt drank her tea at the table. She watched Artie, her eyes crinkling at the corners, as he carried the dishes from the table to the sink. She said we were good, helpful boys. Then she patted the flat of her hand against her chest. She kept patting until, finally, she burped.

"Pardon me," she said.

The phone rang. It was an old-fashioned one with a cord that didn't reach all the way to the table, so Mrs. Burt had to get up.

"You just phoned yesterday," she said to the caller. "What? No. No!"

I felt like I was eavesdropping and, anyway, Artie was grinding his eyes.

"We have to go," I whispered.

She clamped a hand tight over the receiver. "Come over tomorrow, then. We'll go to the bank and get it done." Then she wiggled her fingers at Artie and showed him her scary teeth. He showed his unscary ones back.

On the way to the door I heard her say, "Nobody. Nothing. I'm fine. I am perfectly fine. Quit calling all the time."

5

I FOUND THE checkbook in a drawer in the kitchen. Luckily, a record book was attached so it was easy to figure out the rent. Mom wrote a check to Nelson for the same amount the first day of every month. I did the same, forging her signature again. I was getting good at it. The next morning I stuck it in the metal box in the lobby. Then we went across the street to tell Mrs. Burt.

"They charge that much?" Mrs. Burt said. "You in the penthouse or something?"

"What's a penthouse?" Artie asked, mouth full of toast.

She explained that it was the fanciest apartment at the top of the building.

"We're at the bottom," Artie told Mrs. Burt.

"You sure you don't want eggs?" she asked. "Breakfast is my specialty. You know what I used to do for a living? I was a cook. A cook in a logging camp. A mulligan mixer. That's the slang for it. I can put on a spread like you never seen."

We had eggs, over-easy for me, scrambled for Artie.

After breakfast, Mrs. Burt phoned for a taxi. Artie watched for it out the window and when it showed up, he squealed, "It's *yellow*!" I helped Mrs. Burt down the front steps. Artie carried the walker on his back and the driver put it in the trunk.

Too bad the trip was so short — just up the hill and a few blocks down Broadway where our bank was.

I didn't feel so nervous with an adult. We were even allowed to go straight to the front of the line because of the walker.

"I guess this contraption's good for something," Mrs. Burt whispered.

She took the check and the bills we had to pay out of her purse and explained the whole situation to the teller, about her daughter-in-law being at work and asking her to get it done.

"I got the boys with me today," she said in a fake sweet-old-lady voice. She let go of the walker to put a hand on each of our shoulders.

"Whatever's left, just put it in my daughter-in-law's account," she said, and I almost burst out, "No!"

Outside I told her, "We need the rest of the money, Mrs. Burt. We really need it."

"Don't you worry," she said in her normal not-sweet voice. "I got a plan."

"What?"

"Later. First we got to pick up some food for you growing boys."

We took another taxi to the supermarket because, Mrs. Burt said, the Pit Stop Mart was run by crooks who charged too much and so was the supermarket for that matter, but what could she do? She used to grow her own vegetables, even here in the city, and can or freeze them, but now it was too much work. Now she only grew flowers.

Because she had the grocery cart to keep her steady, she didn't need the walker. Artie stepped between the bars and held it waist-high, the back half dragging along behind him as he clopped and whinnied along the aisles. Mrs. Burt pointed to things and I put them in the cart.

"If you see something you like, tell me," she said. Artie neighed at snack foods he saw on TV and she said, "You don't eat that crap, do you? Oh, I'm going to fix you something better than that."

The cart filled up. It teetered with food and Mrs. Burt paid for it in cash. Then we rolled it out the door and got in the third taxi of our lives and let the man from the supermarket load in all the bags.

 ⟋

MRS. BURT SLID the sandwich off the flipper and onto my plate. "Where'd the pickles get to?"

The things that needed to be in the fridge were already in the fridge, but the rest of the food was all over the counters and the kitchen floor. When we found the pickles, I was the only one strong enough to get the lid off.

"You ready to hear my plan?" Mrs. Burt asked.

My mouth was full of sandwich — ham and cheese dipped in egg and fried like French toast. It was the best sandwich I'd ever had in my life.

"I was going to pay you, right? Instead, how about you come over here to eat and do your laundry? Then you run the errands I need. I scratch your back, you scratch mine. We both got our pride, right? You'll be home to answer the phone if your mother ever calls."

I swallowed and said, "She's going to."

On a scale of one to ten, I ranked her calling a nine.

Mrs. Burt said, "Well, it's a good thing I paid that phone bill then."

That was Saturday. Nelson called again that afternoon to ask where his check was.

"In the box," I told him.

"For cripe's sake, I told her to call me when she put it in."

"She couldn't find the number."

"For cripe's sake!" He slammed the phone down.

FRIED CHICKEN. I don't mean Chancey's Chicken. It didn't even taste like Chancey's. Everything we'd ever eaten that was called fried chicken was not even in the same family as what Mrs. Burt cooked for us. Maybe Chancey was selling fried rats.

"This was pretty popular with the fellas out in the bush," Mrs. Burt told us. "You wouldn't believe how much they ate. I'd stand at that stove cooking and cooking and they wouldn't let me step away for a minute. It was a woodstove, too. Not electric like this. This here is a sissy stove. I'd be chucking in the wood with one hand and frying up the chicken with the other and whipping up another batch of johnnycake with the other."

"That's three hands," I pointed out.

"You're sharp. I needed three hands working up there! Try the johnnycake, Artie."

Artie loved the johnnycake.

"Try the coleslaw," she said.

He did not love the coleslaw. There was dessert, too. Apple cobbler with ice cream.

After supper I helped Mrs. Burt down the basement stairs. I'd brought over our dirty clothes in a pillowcase. She was surprised a boy knew how the washer worked. Then she told us that she used to wash the men's clothes in the logging camp using an old-fashioned wringer washer because there wasn't any electricity.

"I washed their clothes once a season whether they needed it or not. Even the Stanfields." She poked Artie. "That's a joke. They were so filthy they stood up by themselves."

Stanfields were long underwear, she told us.

We went back upstairs, Mrs. Burt very slowly. While we cleaned up, she drank her tea and thumped her chest with the flat of her hand, like she'd done the night before.

Artie asked her why.

"I'm trying to bring up the gas. I get terrible gas after I eat. Here, give me a pat." She leaned forward in the chair so Artie could pat between her shoulder blades.

"Harder."

He patted harder.

"Harder!"

He really whacked her one and Mrs. Burt ribbited like a frog.

"Pardon me!" she said, and we all laughed.

Sunday the menu was pancakes (she called them flapjacks) and sausages for breakfast, and ham and scalloped potatoes for supper and leftover cobbler. For lunch we had flapjack sandwiches. That was Artie's idea. I watered Mrs. Burt's garden and cleaned up the dishes and Artie thumped her on the back. The person who called before called again and Mrs. Burt was just as rude.

Later, at night in our own apartment across the street from Mrs. Burt's house, Artie and I lay together in the hideaway bed listening to Happy tweet his goodnight song to us.

"Tweety, tweety, tweet, tweet! Tweety, tweety, tweet, tweet!"

"Happy's sure happy," I said.

"Me, too," Artie said.

I knew he was happy, because I hadn't had to use to the Economizer Extra-Strength Hand and Body Lotion for two nights in a row. And because, when I put my hands under my pajama top, I felt my stomach round and hard and full. Artie's would feel the same, if he'd let me touch him, which he wouldn't, because he's extremely ticklish. Still, I asked him why.

"Why are you so happy, Artie?" I wanted to hear what he would say about Mrs. Burt's cooking.

"I'm happy because Mom's coming home tomorrow," he said.

Happy went on tweeting above our heads, flying at the end of Artie's arm.

"That's what you said, Curtis. That's what you told Mrs. Gill."

"I said in a *few* days."

"You said two sleeps. I've been counting."

And so I had to tell him about Brandon Penny-packer again. I had to tell him in case Mom *didn't* show up the next morning. Because if she didn't, Artie might tell Mrs. Gill, or some kid at school. Then Social Services would come and take me and Artie away and put us in foster care. And we would be separated.

I was the same age as Artie when I went into foster care. A woman from Social Services came to our apartment to pick me up. I was waiting with Mrs. Gill. Waiting for Mom, who never came home for me.

Through the city, over the bridge, up the side of the mountain. That was where the Pennypackers lived, where trees pressed in all around the houses and even after it stopped raining the water dripped off their shaggy branches for hours. There were no apartment buildings, only houses, all of them with huge garages big enough for two cars. The Pennypackers had two cars. One for Mrs. Pennypacker and one for Mr. Pennypacker, though he was almost never around to drive it because he worked out of town and only came home once a month.

Mrs. Pennypacker welcomed me into their home.

"You are so lucky to be placed here. Because I have my own boy, too. Brandon. He's nine. Brandon!" she called. "You get to share a room with Brandon. He'll be a big brother to you. Brandon!!!!"

It was night and I was tired from everything that had happened that day. Mrs. Pennypacker opened a new toothbrush for me and put on the paste. She showed me which facecloth and towel to use. Then she left me alone.

When I was finished in the bathroom, I opened the door. Right behind it stood a heavy boy in striped pajamas.

Mrs. Pennypacker came up behind him and said, "Oh, good. You've met." She handed me some striped pajamas, which turned out to be exactly the same as Brandon's but in a smaller size.

As soon as I put them on, he said, "Those are mine, you know."

My bed was on the right, Brandon's on the left. There wasn't any nightlight so I cried for a long time in the dark.

Then Brandon said, "Shut up. I can't get to sleep."

I stopped.

"You're an Indian, aren't you?" he said.

"No," I said. Mrs. Gill was an Indian. She was born in India. Her skin was the color of toast and sometimes she came to school dressed in bright Indian tops covered in fancy stitching. I was surprised that Brandon would think I was an Indian when my clothes were so plain.

"The last kid who stayed here was an Indian," Brandon said. "You wouldn't believe what happened to him."

The next morning we had oatmeal for breakfast. Mrs. Pennypacker put on the sugar for us, then took the sugar bowl away. Brandon called for more, but she wouldn't let him have any. It wasn't sweet enough for me, either, but the worst thing was there was something hard like a stone in it. It kept finding its way onto the spoon.

Finally I spat it out into my hand.

"Oh, Curtis!" cried Mrs. Pennypacker. "You've lost a tooth!"

It was the first time it had happened. I started to cry.

"Now the tooth fairy will come. Isn't that lucky? She'll take your tooth and leave you a dollar."

I was glad about the dollar, but it didn't completely cheer me up. Because I missed my mother. Because she wasn't there to see my first tooth come out.

Mrs. Pennypacker walked us to school so she could introduce me to my new teacher. After that I always walked just with Brandon because he was nine and old enough to take me. Usually a lot of kids from the school were walking at the same time, but no one ever walked with us.

On the way home that first day, along the road under the tall dripping trees, Brandon told me that he was the one who made my tooth fall out.

"I have powers," he said. "I can do anything. You better watch out."

At bedtime Mrs. Pennypacker brought me my tooth wrapped in a tissue. She explained that when I was fast asleep, the tooth fairy would fly in the window, take the tooth and leave a dollar for me.

Sure enough, when I woke in the night and felt around under the pillow, my fingers closed around a coin. I clutched it in my hand to keep it safe. I figured I might be able to use it to pay somebody to take me home to my mother.

In the morning, Brandon feeling around under my pillow woke me up. He dashed across to his own bed and threw the covers over himself. When Mrs. Pennypacker came to get us up, I showed her the coin and she clapped her hands and smiled.

As we were leaving the house, Brandon asked to see my dollar.

"Nice," he said, and handed it back.

We walked a different way to school — one that passed by a store. We went in and Brandon filled two little paper bags with penny candy. I wanted some, too, but didn't want to spend the dollar that was going to pay for my rescue if Mom didn't come to get me soon. I hoped Brandon would share his candy, but somehow I knew he wouldn't. I followed him to the counter.

"Can I see your dollar again?" he asked, and I gave it to him. "Go get something, too. I'll pay for it." So I went back and stood for a minute trying to decide what I wanted. Finally I settled on a long red licorice whip.

Brandon had already left the store by then. He was outside in the parking lot tossing candy corns into the air and catching them in his mouth.

"If you say anything to my mom about stopping here," he said, "I'll make the rest of your teeth fall out."

"It wasn't till we got to school," I told Artie, "that I remembered my dollar and asked for it back."

"He spent it, didn't he," Artie said.

"That's right."

Artie sat up, gulping back tears. "He tricked you! He was mean!"

"Really mean," I said. "The meanest kid I ever met. I just hope *you* never have to meet him."

I felt awful saying that.

Because what I was doing to Artie? It was the very same thing Brandon had done to me.

6

THE NEXT NIGHT Mrs. Burt wouldn't even answer the phone when it rang. She said, "It's Marianne — again."

"Who's Marianne?" I asked.

"A big-shot lawyer in Toronto. In other words, a sharpie." Then she added that Marianne was her daughter. I was surprised by the way she said it, the same way she said "telewhatsit." "She wants to sell me out."

"What does that mean?" I asked.

"She wants to put me in a home with a bunch of drooling old people, then sell this place. She'll make a lot of money. Everybody else sold out. I used to have neighbors, but they all went to live in apartments. Then they tore the houses down and threw up these cheap places. There went the neighborhood. But I got my pride."

I didn't say anything. We were living in one of those cheap places.

"The other idea she has," Mrs. Burt went on, "is to pay some nosy person I don't even know to take care of me. You know what I said to her yesterday? I said I had arranged my own help, thank you very much! That's you two boys."

Artie beamed and started patting her on the back. But the gas stayed inside her and she finally sent him away to play in the living-room. Mrs. Burt had shelves full of china figurines — shepherd boys and girls in hoop skirts. She didn't seem to care about them very much because she let a five-and-a-half-year-old with clumsy hands march them around on the coffee table.

I stayed in the kitchen and listened to her complain about her daughter. No wonder she was so grumpy all the time. When she finally ran out of mean things to say, I got up to do the dishes. A couple of times I glanced back and saw her sitting there with fogged-up glasses. I felt sorry for her.

"Police car!" Artie started crowing in the living-room.

It was his favorite thing, along with ambulances, fire trucks and taxis.

"They're getting out of the car!" he sang now. Then he called, "Cur-*tis!* They're going to *our* building!"

I ran to the living-room. Across the street, two officers were buzzing at the intercom. They could have been ringing for somebody else in the building — it sure wasn't the first time the police had come around — but I still felt panicky.

Nobody seemed to be answering.

Then Mrs. Burt appeared and cried, "Duck, boys! Quick!"

We dropped down onto the sofa.

"Stay down," she said. "You don't want them to see you, do you?"

Artie started whimpering, "Are they coming for us?"

Mrs. Burt stuck her jaw in the air. "Help me, Curtis. I'm going over to see what they want."

She went out the back door so I could help her down the steps without being seen.

"Do you think the landlord called them because the rent check bounced?" I asked.

"That's what I'm going to find out," she said, setting off on her own with the walker.

I went back inside. In the living-room, I stepped behind one of the drapes. Artie did the same and together we watched Mrs. Burt hobble out the ABSOLUTELY NO FLYERS! gate. She did a fake double take, like she had just noticed the police. She waved and called out something to them as she crossed the street.

One of the officers went over to her and they talked for a while. I saw Mrs. Burt's expression change. Her glasses slid down her nose. She didn't bother to push them up, just gave her little knitted cap a shake, as though she was sorry about something. Then she nodded to the officer and started back across the street. She didn't look up at the window, even though she knew we were watching.

I went out the back again and waited. At last she limped around the side of the house. She was upset, I could tell, because when she gripped the stair railing and my arm, she held me as tight as that first day I found her stranded on her steps.

"What did they say?" I asked. "Is it the rent? It's the rent, isn't it?"

If Nelson had called the police because our check bounced, they would demand to see our mom. Then all the things I was afraid of would come true.

"Shh," Mrs. Burt said. "I'm thinking."

We went inside again. Slowly, leaning heavily on the walker, Mrs. Burt made it to the living-room.

"Close the drapes," she said.

I closed them and when I turned around, she

had fallen into the big armchair, hands trembling on her knees, still breathing hard.

Finally she lifted her face with the big glasses hanging on the end of her nose.

"Boys?" she said. "This is what I'm thinking. I'm thinking it might be better if you moved in."

WE DECIDED TO wait until night for me to go over and get our things. We couldn't take the chance that somebody would see me going over to Mrs. Burt's.

That's what people in our building always did when they skipped out on the rent — waited for the cover of darkness. It happened a lot. Nelson would haul away anything left behind and stack it beside the dumpster in the underground parking garage for all the rent-paying tenants to pick through. Whatever was left got tossed in the dumpster the night before garbage day. We got a lamp and some dishes that way. Mom was always hoping for a proper bedside table.

Now somebody would get our stuff.

Mrs. Burt said the police would come back because nobody had let them in this time. She advised us not to use her front door anymore and not to walk on the street at all. Maybe we shouldn't even go back to school, she said.

"But what about Mom?" I asked. "How will she know where we are?"

"We'll keep an eye out for her," Mrs. Burt said. "And whatever you do, *don't* leave a note. It could fall into the wrong hands."

"The landlord, you mean?"

"Or the police. They'll come over here and bust the door in!" She started thumping her chest, like they were already bursting in and giving her a heart attack.

When it was Artie's bedtime, Mrs. Burt showed us two bedrooms. Artie started to cry and I explained that we slept in the same bed, which made the choice easy because there was a double bed in one of the rooms and a twin in the other. Artie still wouldn't stop. He was scared of all the commotion, of things changing so fast.

I asked Mrs. Burt what kind of hand lotion she used, and after I explained she pointed to the bathroom and said to take what I needed.

She kept saying, "You poor dear. Oh, you little darling. I'm so sorry. I really am."

After what had happened with the baby lotion at the Pit Stop Mart, I knew it was no use even trying with her cold cream.

Mrs. Burt thought of the figurines. It took half an hour for Artie to transfer them all from the living-room to the bedroom and get them organized the way he wanted. Then there was cookies and milk and the fun of toothbrushing with his finger.

As soon as we lay down in the strange bed, in the room that smelled like nobody had slept in it for a million years, he fell asleep. A thick curtain kept out most of the light, but around its edges I could tell it wasn't dark yet. I didn't feel like going out and sitting with Mrs. Burt when I was so upset. I was as upset as Artie, but too old to cry about it, though I felt like it.

The police would come back to evict us. We'd seen it happen before. Except we wouldn't be there. We would be hiding out at Mrs. Burt's, so they would never find out that we were on our own. They would think we'd skipped out with Mom.

And we weren't on our own anymore anyway. We had Mrs. Burt. But what about when Mom came back? How could I let her know we were just across the street? How could I let her know we were still waiting and seven out of ten positive she still loved us?

When the outline of light around the curtain disappeared, I came out of the bedroom. Mrs. Burt had a bunch of pillowcases ready for me.

"Just take what you really want and need," she said. "We can pick up new stuff. And don't forget that lotion."

I felt like a burglar.

Lights were on in most of the apartments except ours. I waited in Mrs. Burt's yard while a few cars passed, then ran across the street.

I unlocked the lobby door and used the little key to check the mail. Flyers spilled out. I left them on the floor.

As soon as I was inside our apartment, I switched on the light and started madly stuffing school things in one pillowcase and clothes in another. I went to the bathroom and threw in our toothbrushes and the Economizer Extra-Strength Hand and Body Lotion. In Mom's room, the silk eye mask was lying on the cardboard box. I did that thing Artie always did — I stroked my face with it — but instead of making me feel better, I felt worse. So I left it there. I lifted the cardboard box and grabbed her wallet just to have the I.D. card from the community college with her picture on it.

Then I lifted the box again, because from the corner of my eye I'd noticed something.

The ring box. The ring box that held my tooth. It was under there, too. I picked it up, and right away I knew how I could leave a message that only she could find. I knew because wherever she was, eventually she would come back, even if we weren't here.

She would come for that tooth.

I wrote a note.

Mom, we love you. We are across the street staying with the old lady. We are waiting for you.

I tucked it inside the ring box.

The first place Mom would check would be where the tooth had been in the first place, under her cardboard box bedside table. But Nelson would clear out our stuff and somebody else would move in, so I pushed the box aside and pulled up the carpet. It came up easily. On the foam underpad, over and over so the message would be clear, I wrote: *Look for the tooth*.

Where do you brush your teeth?

In the bathroom, I wrote.

I taped the ring box in the cupboard under the sink. You had to either reach your hand up and feel around for it, or get on your knees and stick your head right inside the cupboard.

Who would do that? Only a person looking hard for something. Only a person looking for the single valuable thing she owned in all the world.

THAT NIGHT BRANDON Pennypacker was in my dream. It was supper at the Pennypackers and he was carrying my plate to me at the table. On the way, he stopped and turned his back. When he turned around again, there was a shiny string of spit attaching his lip to the food, like a spider web that stretched and broke as he set the plate in front of me.

It was just a bad dream, but one that had really happened in real life almost every single night.

The next day was the Wednesday of the last week of school. The smell of bacon woke me up.

At first I didn't know where I was. Artic, though, was his old self, and bacon was one of the things his old self liked best. He bounded off to Mrs. Burt's kitchen. I got there last.

Mrs. Burt was at the stove wearing a man's dressing gown and, for the first time, no cap. Her white hair floated around her head like dandelion fuzz. She looked so puffy and clutched the walker so hard that I knew she'd had about as good a sleep as I had.

"Boys," she said, settling at the table with us to drink her tea. "I have an idea. How about a day off school?" To me she said, "I think we should take turns keeping an eye out. See what happens across the street."

"How many more sleeps till Mom comes home?" Artie asked between spoonfuls of scrambled eggs.

"Who knows?" Mrs. Burt said. "Today might be the day." And she shot me a sideways glance to let me know she was stringing him along. "We don't want her walking into that hornet's nest, do we? The police casing the place. She could get into some real trouble over that rent money."

After breakfast, I washed the dishes while Mrs. Burt got dressed and took her position at the living-room window, the drapes open just a slit. Artie was already dressed because he'd slept in his clothes. While he played with Happy and the figurines on the living-room floor, he kept telling Mrs. Burt, "You should sleep in your clothes, too. Then you don't have to get dressed in the morning!"

I came in and Mrs. Burt said, "Good. My neck's getting stiff." Then it was my turn for guard duty. She hobbled off to her room to lie down.

They showed up just before lunchtime while Mrs. Burt was in the kitchen making sandwiches. The police car pulled up with two officers in it. After that another car arrived and a man got out.

It was Nelson, the landlord. He went over and shook hands with the officers. Then the three of them walked together to the apartment.

Mrs. Burt was suddenly right behind me with a plate in her hand.

"Oh!" she cried and dropped the plate so the sandwiches bounced onto the floor and broke open. Meat and lettuce and bread flew everywhere.

"Did they go in?"

"Yes," I said.

Mrs. Burt handed me the empty plate and eased herself down on the coffee table. She slapped her chest twice like she was trying to bring up her words.

"Actually, boys? I've been thinking." She paused to belch into her fist. "See, I have a place. A cabin. It's quite far away and I haven't been there for years. It's a beautiful place on a lake." She stopped again and I saw that her eyes had teared up behind the glasses. "Would you like to see it? I won't force you or nothing. You can come on a little holiday with me or you can go across the street and let them know what's up."

"I want to go on a holiday," Artie piped up.

Mrs. Burt's speckled hand clutched her chest. She turned to me.

"What about you, Curtis?"

I thought about Mom and how she would find us. If we left, the note I'd written her would be useless. No one would answer the door at Mrs. Burt's.

I turned and looked out the window again at the police car, burning white in the sun. When I shut my eyes, I could still see it taking away all our choices.

I turned back to Mrs. Burt and said we'd go with her.

7

THE REST OF that day we got ready. Artie and I went around closing all the drapes and curtains. We moved most of the food we'd bought down to the basement freezer. Mrs. Burt did other things like cancel the newspaper and write checks.

"It's too bad about the garden," she said. "But I guess it had already gone to pot. Get it? Gone to *flower* pots?" She laughed.

Gerry used to laugh at his own jokes like that when he was drunk. Now that we were leaving, Mrs. Burt seemed drunk.

Artie and I brought all the houseplants out to the back yard where they would at least get rained on from time to time. I soaked them with the hose. Mrs. Burt said Artie could bring along two of the figurines. He eeny-meeny-miney-moed and ended up choosing a little boy in the branch of an apple tree and a girl in a pink dress holding a white kitten. With newspaper and a shoebox, he made a nest and snuggled them in with Happy.

Then came a big surprise. A good surprise.

Mrs. Burt had a car.

When everything was piled outside by the back gate, Mrs. Burt locked the door behind us. She asked me to open the doors of the old wooden garage out back. They squawked. Daylight streamed inside. You couldn't miss the car, which was under a blue tarp.

"Go ahead, boys," Mrs. Burt said. "Be my guest." Artie and I each grabbed a corner of the tarp and started walking backwards until we'd pulled it off.

Blue and white. The blue of a robin's egg, with a chrome bumper that matched the walker. Fins at the back where the lights were set. A big, old-fashioned car.

"What you're looking at here, boys," Mrs. Burt said, "is the handsomest vehicle ever to drive off an assembly line. A 1957 Chevy Bel Air."

We piled inside — Artie and me, I mean. Mrs. Burt just stood in the alley laughing and showing her brown teeth while we bounced around and took turns pretending to drive. Then she got serious and said we'd better hustle or we'd be on the highway after dark. Holding onto the car instead of the walker, she went around and opened the hood. With a flashlight from a shelf behind us, she shone a light inside.

"What are you doing?" I asked when she passed me the flashlight to hold.

"I only drive it a couple times a year, so I always disconnect the battery. I hope she runs."

It started fine. The engine hummed a little song. I loaded everything into the trunk, including the walker, then folded the tarp up and left it on the shelf like Mrs. Burt asked.

The last thing we did before we left town was head for a car wash.

"I can't stand a dirty car," Mrs. Burt told us. "If you wash and wax a car, it stays pretty. If you look after its working parts, it lasts. Except for these." She waved a hand at the cars all around us waiting for the light to change. "These cars are made to fall apart. Also, they're ugly and they all look the same."

Sitting high in the passenger seat, I agreed with her. The other drivers seemed to, too. When the light turned green and she put on the signal to change lanes, cars made way for her. People turned their heads and smiled.

Mrs. Burt said, "Hunker down a little, Curtis. Don't sit up there so proud. We're on the lam, remember?"

I slid down in the seat. "What's on the lam?"

"We're absconding. We're getting away."

We pulled into a gas station. Mrs. Burt gave me money and told me to fill the tank and pay for a wash as well.

"I want to help!" Artie piped up from the back seat.

"You stay right there," Mrs. Burt told him. She used the same sweet voice she fooled bank tellers with. "I don't think it's a good idea for you two to be seen together. Not till we're out of town, anyway."

I'd never gassed up a car before. Luckily, the instructions were right on the pump. Then I wished somebody from school could see me filling the Bel Air. I wished Mr. Bryant could because then he'd ask me about it. Whenever something special happened to somebody, he made sure everybody knew, and because it was him insisting you tell, you didn't have to feel like you were bragging about it.

No one did see me, though, because we were already far from our neighborhood and, anyway, the school year was over for me.

I came back with the receipt, smiling because the attendant had complimented me on the car.

Then Artie asked, "Is this where Mom works?"

It felt like a slap.

"No," I told Artie. "She worked at Pay-N-Save. This is Shell."

We drove around the side of the building to the car wash. The man who took the receipt gave her a thumbs up, meaning the car was a beauty. Mrs. Burt shut the engine off and told us to roll up the windows tight.

I felt us jerk forward. Slowly, we were pulled through the big opening in the wall. In the darkness ahead I could just make out the brushes hanging down like seaweed. Artie whimpered at the sound of the machinery, but then jets of water started firing all around us like a thousand water pistols and he laughed. Mrs. Burt caught the giggles next. Then I did. I couldn't help it.

Soap splatted down on us.

"Seagulls!" I yelled and we all screamed as the brushes whirred to life. They closed around us on all sides, scrubbing and whipping up the suds. Soon we were completely covered in foam, which seemed even funnier than the water jets. It was like being trapped inside a huge lemon meringue pie.

A tidal wave of clean water splashed over us.

"Wheee!" Artie shrieked. It splashed us again and again. Then a typhoon of hot air dried us off.

The sign by the exit flashed START YOUR ENGINE NOW, and before we knew it we were belched out just like Mrs. Burt's gas.

"Let's do it again!" Artie screamed.

Mrs. Burt drove out onto the street. The car gleamed in the afternoon sun and water droplets flew off the hood like sparks. I unrolled the window and let the June air wash my face.

Mrs. Burt did the same, unrolling her window and shouting out for all the world to hear, "We're absconding, boys! We're absconding! Yippee!"

THE NAME OF the first town that we stopped at was Hope.

"My thingie," Mrs. Burt said, and I unloaded the walker from the trunk and brought it to her. With a lot of groaning, she got out from behind the wheel. She let me and Artie top up the gas together this time.

I checked the oil, too. She showed me how. When all that was done, she suggested some supper in the diner attached to the gas station, since it would be a long time before our next stop. We had a whole bunch of mountains to drive across.

I took Artie to the bathroom and when we

came back Mrs. Burt was already settled in a booth where three paper placemats with frilly edges were laid out. Artie slid in next to Mrs. Burt. I took the facing window seat. Outside, big trucks were roaring past. I could see a wide gray river between the trees. The town was sitting right at the bottom of a mountain, in its shadow, so it already seemed like it was getting dark.

The waitress came with menus and a jar of broken crayons for Artie to decorate the placemats. He pointed in the menu at the colored picture of bacon and eggs.

"You already had breakfast," I said. "This is supper."

But Mrs. Burt said, "Breakfast at suppertime! It makes you feel like you're starting the day fresh. Let's start all over again, boys. Let's forget all that fuss this morning. Remember, we're in Hope!"

By "fuss" she meant the police. I'd actually forgotten them until she brought it up. As soon as she did, I felt hopeless. Hopeless about Mom and how to let her know where we were.

The waitress came back with Mrs. Burt's tea and a saucer piled with plastic creamers. After she left, Artie drank the creamers. Mrs. Burt let him. When the waitress came back with our orders balanced along her arm, Mrs. Burt pushed the saucer of empty creamers toward her and said, "We'll need more of these."

The waitress didn't blink an eye. She brought more at the same time she brought a little silver rack filled with individual portions of jam and honey and peanut butter. Artie forgot about the creamers because he'd never seen anything as wonderful as this little rack.

"It's a walker for jam!" he said. He was so busy emptying it and restacking the jams, he couldn't focus on his food until I suggested he try all the different jams on his toast. Mrs. Burt tipped what was left in the rack into her purse.

Waving her arm, she called out to the waitress, "We need more jam over here, miss!"

This time the waitress did blink. She blinked and frowned, but Mrs. Burt stared her down until she went away and came back with more jam.

Artie, I realized then, was going to be a very spoiled kid before all this was over.

After breakfast number two, we drove on. Mrs. Burt leaned close to the wheel, staring out through her glasses and the windshield, thumping her chest and burping all the way.

We were taking the old highway. On the new highway you had to pay a toll. Also, the old highway was more picturesque, she said. It wound above the river, higher and higher, curvier and curvier.

Soon I began to feel like throwing up. Partly I was worried about leaving Mom behind. Partly it was carsickness. Car after car passed us, even on those dangerous bends, which was maybe the real reason she took the old highway. The Bel Air couldn't make the speed limit when we were going uphill.

Artie and I dozed off. When we were all awake again, Mrs. Burt taught Artie a song called "I've Heard That Song Before," which they sang over and over until I had to say, "I've heard it before, too. Like about a million times." I peeled the covers off one jam after another and passed them to Artie in the back seat. He couldn't sing when he was licking jam out of the little packets.

It was almost dark when we finally drove down from the mountains into a bald, hilly countryside. Mrs. Burt took the exit after a big sign that read MOTOR HOTEL and was pleased to see trucks filling the parking lot.

"You can always tell a motel has a good bed, or a restaurant has good grub, if truckers stop there," Mrs. Burt told us.

Very slowly, very stiffly, she hobbled into the office with the walker I'd got from the trunk. We waited in the car until she came back a few minutes later carrying a key on a wooden block.

The room had brown carpet and two double beds separated by a night table.

"Well, looky here, boys," she said, going over to one of the beds. "This is a bonus."

There was a metal box attached to the headboard with a slot on the top for coins. The instructions were printed on it, but it never said what the box did. Mrs. Burt knew.

"It's a vibrator bed."

"What's that?" I asked.

First she made us change into our pajamas and brush our teeth. Then she asked me to read the instructions because the print was too small for her.

"Twenty-five cents for ten minutes. Fifty cents for half an hour."

"Half an hour's the better deal." She fished in her purse for a quarter for each of us and we fed them to the box.

A noise started up as loud as the car wash, and the bed began to tremble. I thought it was an earthquake until Mrs. Burt cried, "Lie down, boys! Lie down!" Artie and I fell onto our backs laughing and let the bed shake us like jumping beans.

"Get on, Mrs. Burt!" Artie cried and she did. She fell down next to us and we all jiggled together.

It would have been relaxing if it wasn't so loud. I guess that was the "motor" part in Motor Hotel.

We fell asleep with the lights on and the vibrator bed still rumbling. The last thing Artie said was, "Mrs. Burt? This was the best day of my life."

BANG, BANG, BANG!

I sat up. Between the bangs, it seemed very quiet. The bed had shut off. The room was dark, but I could still see because the lights from the motel office shone through the curtain.

"Georgina!" somebody shouted just as the pounding started again. "Georgina! Open up!"

Artie clutched me. In the other bed, Mrs. Burt was feeling around on the bedside table for her glasses. Once she got them on her face, she peered across at us. When she saw we were awake, she switched on the light.

"Georgina!" the man at the door bellowed.

"There's no Georgina here!" Mrs. Burt bellowed back. "Go to bed!"

"Like hell! Come out!"

At the sound of that swear word, Mrs. Burt really woke up. She snatched the walker waiting by the bed and struggled to her feet. Barefoot and in her nightie, she stomped over to the door. Even on carpet you could hear she was mad just by the way she put the walker down.

"Watch your language," she said through the door. "I got kids in here."

"Get out here, Georgina," the man roared.

"You'll be sorry if I open up this door!"

"Don't open the door!" Artie wailed.

"Mrs. Burt!" I said. "Get back!"

She did not. She undid the chain. When she threw the door open, she had to lean into the frame for support while her other hand shoved the walker out.

There was a very drunk man outside swaying all over the place. I knew he was drunk because of Gerry. Sometimes Gerry had to pee in the bathtub because he couldn't hit the toilet when he was swaying so much. That was how drunk this man looked. Gerry-drunk.

Mrs. Burt wasn't that much steadier. She took a wobbly step forward and knocked the walker against his legs.

He stumbled back.

"Where's Georgina?" he slurred.

"I told you, she isn't here. Now leave us alone. I got a couple of kids with me. We don't like your bad language."

He rubbed his eyes and looked at her, all confused — Mrs. Burt in her nightie with her dandelion hair, just the walker between them. Artie was bawling by then.

When I appeared in the doorway, the man looked from Mrs. Burt to me and hiccuped.

"Excuse me, ma'am. I got the wrong room."

"You sure do," said Mrs. Burt.

"I apologize."

"I should hope so."

I closed the door and put the chain on again and offered my arm so Mrs. Burt could get back to bed a little quicker. Between calling out to Artie, "There, there. That bad man went away and Mrs. Burt is here. Nobody got hurt. You're safe with Mrs. Burt," she was chuckling to herself.

"I want my mom," Artie cried.

Mrs. Burt sat on our bed. "Of course you do."

I got the lotion from the pillowcase, and Mrs. Burt watched me dry Artie's face with the sheet and smooth it on.

THE NEXT MORNING at breakfast Artie stayed tight against Mrs. Burt in the restaurant booth. Mrs. Burt told us she'd been so excited after chasing Georgina's boyfriend away that she couldn't stop shaking. She thought the vibrator bed had turned back on.

"Do you see, boys? I don't take guff from any-body. I don't care how big and strong they are." She slurped her tea. "I know how to handle men, especially. The bigger and stronger the better. You should have seen me cooking in those camps. I was the only woman mulligan mixer. The only woman for a hundred miles."

But I wasn't really listening. I was thinking about how to let Mom know we'd gone.

There were only two things I could do: write and phone. I knew that on a scale of one to ten her answering the phone this morning would be about a one, but I had to try. Because when we were back together again — me and Mom and Artie — I wanted to be able to say to her that I'd done everything I could.

"Mrs. Burt? Could I borrow some money?"

"Sure," she said, opening her purse and sliding ten dollars across the table to me. Then, since the purse was already open in her lap, she dumped in all the jams from the rack.

"Get some snacks for the road," she said.

"I'm getting change for the phone," I said.

Her face fell so hard it almost hit the table. She grabbed my hand.

"If somebody else answers, hang up. Okay, Curtis? Hang up." And from how her fingers dug in, she put fear in me.

"Okay," I said.

At the cash register I changed the ten for quarters. Then I went to the lobby where the pay phone was. The number was long distance. A little message popped up telling me how much money to put in.

As the phone started to ring, the hope in me started to rise. It rang and rang and rang. Then all of the quarters jangled down into the coin return slot and the ringing stopped.

WE DROVE THROUGH the town and out into the scrubby hills. Mrs. Burt said we were still heading north. In the back seat, Artie played with Happy and the china figurines while I watched out the window. Sometimes there were cows.

I started to feel like I was watching a movie on TV. Even though there weren't any characters, there was action. We were escaping! And the countryside was changing. The desert hills flattened out and got greener. Farms and towns appeared and disappeared. The forest spread out across the land.

I asked Mrs. Burt about the car, and she said that Mr. Burt had bought it new in 1957.

"Where is Mr. Burt?" Artie asked.

"He's deceased. Do you know what that means?"

"He has rickets?"

"Not diseased. *Deceased*. He's dead."

Artie started to wail. It seemed out of the blue, but probably wasn't. You never know what's going on in a little kid's head. Maybe all this time he'd been thinking of what I had been trying so hard not to think.

That Mom was dead. That that was why she never came home.

"Don't worry," Mrs. Burt said. "It was a long time ago. He's in heaven. I think."

"Where's my mom?" Artie asked. "Where is she?"

Mrs. Burt turned to me. "Should I pull over?"

I told her to keep driving. Then I undid my seatbelt and crawled over the back of the seat to be with Artie. That's something you can do in a big old car like a Bel Air.

To change the subject, Mrs. Burt asked Artie if he wanted to hear about his namesake, King Arthur, and the sword in the stone. Hundreds of years ago, in England, a wizard put it there.

"Only the true king of England would be able to pull that sword out. Everybody tried. They tugged away on the thing, grunting and groaning, but it wouldn't budge. Then this boy by the name of Arthur — Artie for short — swaggered up and just plucked the darn thing out. What do you think of that?"

"I like it," Artie said.

"He got together some knights who would meet at a big stone table in the woods. It was round, which was why they were called the Knights of the Round Table. Around this table the knights planned their deeds."

"What are deeds?"

"Brave acts."

"Like what you did, Mrs. Burt," Artie said. "Like when you chased that man away with your walker."

Mrs. Burt got a big chuckle out of that.

We stopped for lunch, which was breakfast again. Before we got back in the car, Mrs. Burt got Artie to thump her back. She said the grease was killing her. But it wasn't killing her enough to order something besides breakfast.

Just before suppertime, we arrived in a big town.

"Ho, ho," she said, peering all around. "Has this place ever changed." Rather than check right into a motel, we drove around so she could exclaim over and over that everything had gone to pot.

"There used to be a store right here on Main Street where you could buy everything you needed. Dishes. Kerosene. Dried beans. Flour. Canoe paddles. It was what we called a dry goods store. You ever heard of that?"

"No," we said.

"You got your stuff on credit. That meant you didn't have to pay up front. But not like with a credit card, where they charge interest. It was an honor system. I would order all the stuff we needed for the camp. I'd sign the book. Mr. Taggart would ship it off to me. At the end of the season when the logs were all bought up and there was money, Taggart would get paid. Everybody got paid. We knew each other and everybody was honest. Not like today."

We drove all the way to the end of the street, but there was no Taggart's Store. What there was was a huge mall with a Canadian Tire and a supermarket.

Mrs. Burt sniffed and said that was what the world had come to: tires and shopping carts.

The motel we stayed in that night was right in town. There wasn't any vibrator bed.

That night Mrs. Burt was so excited about

seeing the cabin the next day that her gas got really bad. Artie sat behind her on the bed pounding his fists between her shoulder blades so hard I thought she would be all bruised. Now and then a tiny burp escaped and Artie would yell, "Good job, Mrs. Burt! There's another one!"

I told them about that kid in my class, Mickey Roach, who could burp the alphabet.

"How?" Artie asked.

"He just says it in burps. I don't know how."

"Try it, Mrs. Burt!" Artie said as he pounded.

"I got my pride!" she said.

"Nobody can hear you," I said.

She turned all serious and her glasses slipped down her nose. We could tell she was about to burp again because she always puffed her cheeks out just before.

"A," she said. It sounded deep and hollow, like she'd burped in a cave. Artie and I burst out laughing and she did, too, her shoulders shaking. Then another burp escaped all on its own, sounding like "B." We screamed. When she burped C, we screamed louder. She had to get a tissue from the bathroom to wipe her eyes, we were laughing so hard.

"Do you understand now, boys, why I can't ever go into an old folks' home? Who would help me with my gas?"

"The nurses," I said.

"Ha. They won't. They'll put me in diapers and leave me in the corner."

"You're too old for diapers, Mrs. Burt," Artie said.

"Darn right I am."

"Who patted your back before we came along?" I asked her.

"Nobody," Mrs. Burt said. "It was very painful."

We got quiet after she said that. Even Artie understood how sad it was that Mrs. Burt lived all alone, far from her daughter the Big Shot who just wanted to put her in a home for old people and not help her with her gas. He wrapped his skinny arms around her and Mrs. Burt squeezed him back.

In a quavery voice, she told us, "But I got you now, don't I? We're helping each other out."

8

THAT NIGHT I called Mom again from the motel pay phone before I went to bed. I also bought a postcard from the front desk that showed a picture of the town. It didn't have much writing space, so I stuck to the important stuff. That we loved her, that we were fine, that we'd left with Mrs. Burt so we wouldn't be separated by Social Services.

They didn't have stamps at the front desk so I gave the card to Mrs. Burt to mail.

I called the next day, too, from the mall before we left. When I got no answer, I asked Mrs. Burt if there was a phone at the cabin.

She said, "I, for one, will be glad to get somewhere where there isn't a phone ringing all the time."

"Did you mail my postcard?"

"Yes, I did."

We bought so much stuff, or Mrs. Burt did.

Food, towels, life jackets, sleeping bags. A mop, a broom, a bucket. Rolls of screening. Mosquito coils. Toilet paper. A kettle, not the plug-in kind. An ax.

But the best thing she bought were two fishing rods, which she just handed to Artie and me.

"Here you go, boys. I hope you catch something." The Bel Air was stuffed to the ceiling — really — when we drove away. By then we were as excited as she was.

On the highway out of town, huge trucks rumbled past us, stacked with logs. Mrs. Burt stuck out her tongue at them. She said they were ruining the forests the way they logged today. They mowed down every tree but only hauled away the big ones, leaving the rest to rot. Later somebody would come by and supposedly plant new trees, but that was no replacement, she said, for Mother Nature.

"In my day they only cut the best logs. That gave the smaller trees a chance to grow. Now they're so greedy they just chop, chop, chop."

To find the turn-off she asked for our sharp eyes. There would be two big boulders on either side of the road — one with a rusty old-fashioned saw blade propped against it.

We managed to find the boulders after driving past them once. Mrs. Burt had to make a U-turn in the middle of the highway when she realized we'd gone too far. There they were, almost completely overgrown with grass. There wasn't any saw.

"Stolen," she said with a snort.

You could hardly call it a road. It was more like a really bumpy lane. The Bel Air bounced along the ruts, crashed over shrubs. Everything inside, including us, shook like a baby rattle.

"Whee!" Artie cried, and I decided I would never go on a ride at the PNE again. After the automatic car wash, the vibrator bed, and now bouncing through the forest in a 1957 Chevy Bel Air with sleeping bags and fishing rods and mosquito nets falling on our heads — it just wouldn't seem that great.

Eventually we had to stop because Mrs. Burt was afraid the Bel Air's suspension would be ruined. I was afraid I'd throw up.

Artie took the shoebox that held the figurines and Happy. Mrs. Burt, though she stuffed as much as she could in her purse, needed both her hands free for the walker. I put a bottle of water in the hotdog pocket of my pants and the ax handle through a belt loop, then slung two bags over my shoulders. We started walking.

It was cool in the shade of the trees and quiet except for the concert the birds were putting on.

The air smelled so sweet it was almost sticky.

"It's grown so much!" Mrs. Burt exclaimed. "The size of the trees! I can't believe it! They were barely this big the last time I was here!" She held her thumb out.

"Are we lost?" Artie asked.

"Not at all. We're following this road all the way to the cabin."

"How long till we're there?"

Mrs. Burt lifted the walker and set it down carefully just ahead of her.

"At this rate, a while. But then we can rest up. It's your poor brother who's got to lug all that stuff from the car."

I didn't mind. I didn't mind at all.

"In the old days," Mrs. Burt said, "we drove right in."

"How long since you've been here, Mrs. Burt?" I asked.

"A long time. More than forty years. Marianne used to come with her dad after that. When she got too old, he'd come himself. For the fishing."

"Why didn't you come?" I asked. "Don't you like fishing?"

"What are you talking about? I used to catch the biggest trout in the lake. That would make him so mad! Mr. Burt, I mean. He'd sit in that canoe for hours and only bring up these puny things. I'd drop my line and some great whopper'd jump right on." She laughed. "I'll show you. I got fish sense."

"I want to catch a fish," Artie told her.

"You will. I promise."

I thought it was strange that she liked fishing so much but wouldn't come here with Mr. Burt. Then I realized they had probably divorced. Maybe they'd divorced over fishing.

"I hope the place is okay," she said. "It's going to be dirty, that's for sure. I hope nobody busted the windows out."

We stopped for a rest and a drink of water. Artie leaned against a tree and ate some jam. I could tell that Mrs. Burt was nervous because she started to thump her chest and burp.

After a half hour of walking, something shiny appeared far ahead through the trees. Mrs. Burt stopped when she saw it, and right away tears were pouring down her cheeks. Artie put down his shoebox and flung himself at her, hugging her thick waist, almost knocking her and the contraption over. She took off her glasses and wiped them, but the tears wouldn't stop.

"Blast it!" she said. "I'm sorry, boys. I'm sorry." She gestured with her chin toward the shiny thing between the trees. "That's the lake."

"Are you happy crying or sad crying?" Artie asked, still clinging to her.

She looked down at him. "I'm happy crying now."

As we got closer, the road started to dip and the trees thinned out and I could see that it was water, a giant, sparkling bowl of it. It was late morning and getting hotter, even under the trees.

Mrs. Burt read my mind.

"Curtis, can you swim?"

"I'm a really good swimmer. We get free lessons in the summer."

"What about Artie?"

"He's scared," I said.

"I am not!" said Artie.

"He can't *ever* go in without a life jacket," Mrs. Burt said. "Do you understand?"

The cabin came into view.

"There it is!" she cried. "Still standing! We got a place to live!"

Artie and I rushed ahead and tried to look inside. The windows were too grimy to see through and the curtains were closed. Mrs. Burt caught up and jiggled the padlock that hung off the door latch. Her fingers came away powdered with rust.

"Isn't it funny," she said. "I can still remember where we used to hide that key." She walked around the other side of the cabin, leaving the walker behind, dragging her hand along the wall for support. Above her head was a small window.

She felt around on the sill, then looked confused, like maybe she misremembered after all. Artie squatted at her feet and picked something off the ground.

The key.

It didn't work. The rusted key wouldn't fit the rusted lock, but I had the ax. She asked me to use the flat end. After a few smashes, the whole latch tore right off the doorframe.

I was first to see inside. Everything that could be torn apart was — torn apart so badly I couldn't even tell what it was supposed to be. The stove was there and some wooden furniture, but everything else was all over the floor, shredded and scattered. Not only that, the place reeked.

Mrs. Burt gasped and her knees gave way and she started to sink. I grabbed her just in time, gripping under her arms and easing her to the ground.

"Oh!" she moaned, covering her face. "I wish we'd never come! Who would do such a thing? People are no good! They're no good! I always said so!"

Her wailing set Artie wailing, too.

I was still in shock about the mess, but not nearly as shocked as I was by what happened next.

From inside came a thumping sound, then some high-pitched squeals. Before I could turn to look, a drumming started up like fingers imitating the gallop of horses. Like a hundred tiny horses, they poured out the cabin door. I looked down and saw a furry stream running between and around my legs. Both Artie and Mrs. Burt stopped wailing and gaped along with me.

"Squirrels!" Mrs. Burt cried, clapping her hands. "Squirrels!"

They vanished in a second. It would have been hard to believe what we'd seen if it wasn't for the wrecked inside of the cabin. Mrs. Burt laughed and I helped her up again, which was hard, partly because she was laughing so hard. Artie was already hiding behind a tree.

"You can come out, Artie," I called. "They're gone."

"No!"

Mrs. Burt brushed herself off. Using the doorframe to steady herself, she took a brave step inside. She couldn't get very far.

"Boys, it's been years since we used to come here. Yet nobody's touched it! No person, I mean. It shows you. People around here are decent."

"Even though the squirrels aren't," I said.

Artie shouted out from behind the tree, "Squirrels are no good!"

IT TOOK HOURS to clear out the cabin. We emptied it and burned most of the stuff. Artie and I did. Mrs. Burt sat on a rock and told us what to do. Rip down the curtains and burn them. Burn the rugs. Burn any books that had been chewed up, which was most of them.

There were two bedrooms in the cabin. We burned the old clothes that were in the drawers there, all the bedding, and the mattresses that were half-shredded and full of ants and smelled like pee.

In one of the bedrooms I found an old wooden Coca-Cola crate with a board nailed over the top, but when I came out of the cabin carrying it, Mrs. Burt shouted, "Not that! Put it down." I set it by the corner of the cabin, away from the giant mountain of junk we had piled up.

When the cabin was empty except for the table and chairs and the stove, we set fire to all the junk. We were careful to stack it away from the cabin where there was a natural clearing. Even so, Mrs.

Burt made us haul water in a bucket from the lake and soak the ground all around first.

Then she took the kerosene that we'd found in a rusty can and splashed it on. She and I went to opposite sides of the pile with the matches.

In a burst it lit, flames shooting high. Horrible black smoke gushed, full of fluttering ash.

"Step back," she told us.

From a safe distance, her hands gripping the walker, she stared as all those things from her past burned. I thought she would be sad. She was frowning, but the lenses of her glasses reflected the fire and seemed to sparkle, as though she was glad, too.

After the fire had burned down, she had us pour buckets of water over the ashes, just in case. Then she told us we looked like a couple of chimney sweeps. I didn't know what she meant, but I was happy because she let us strip and jump in the water without the life jackets, which were still in the Bel Air. At the shoreline the water wasn't too deep and Mrs. Burt waded in and stayed next to Artie.

Later she marched us out and made us stand in the trees to soap ourselves. This was to keep soap out of the lake. The lake was going to be everything for us, she said. Drinking water, bathtub, where we got our food. We had to keep it clean.

So we rinsed off in the trees with buckets of water tipped over our soapy heads. She let us go back in the lake if we promised to stay near shore. Even then she stood and watched us the whole time.

While we were splashing around, Artie spotted a canoe. It followed a curved line from the end of the lake, coming closer, fast. Mrs. Burt hurried us out and gathered us behind her like a mother hen.

A stranger glided in, his wooden canoe making a scraping sound as it bumped up on the shore. He was old, with a beard and a leather hat stained darker where he had sweated through it. His face looked leathery, too. Artie stiffened next to me, because of the beard.

For a moment Mrs. Burt and the man just stared at each other. Then, slowly, the man seemed to recognize Mrs. Burt.

"Mavis?"

"That isn't Spar Munro," Mrs. Burt answered.

"It is," he said and she started laughing. The old man smiled back with teeth worse than Mrs. Burt's. "I saw smoke. Thought the place was on fire."

"We're clearing out the junk."

"Ah," he said, looking at us wrapped in towels behind Mrs. Burt. "Those Marianne's kids?"

"Yes," she said. "Boys, this is an old friend, Mr. Munro. You still living out here or just summering now?"

"Living."

"Want to step out?" she asked.

"I can see you're busy. Maybe another time."

"You been keeping an eye on this place, Spar?"

"Sort of. I only had to drive people away once or twice."

"Well, I thank you," said Mrs. Burt.

"There were squirrels!" Artie exclaimed, and Mr. Munro laughed and waved with the big leather glove of his hand. Pushing off the bottom with the paddle, he about-faced the canoe and slipped away as fast as he came.

As soon as he was out of earshot, Mrs. Burt said, "Doesn't he look old, boys? Ancient! How old would you say he is?"

"Twenty-nine," Artie guessed.

"Come on! He looks about eighty to me. He's not even seventy, I'm pretty sure of that, cause he's younger than me." She straightened her knitted cap and patted it with both hands. "Also, he can't count. Marianne's kids? Ha! If Marianne had kids they'd be all grown up!"

After I unloaded most of the Bel Air, which took about a hundred trips, I got my first wood-chopping lesson.

Mrs. Burt poked along the edge of the trees until she found a fallen log she liked. I dragged it up on two stones and cut it into same-size lengths with the saw. Mrs. Burt called this "bucking." Then we found a nice flat rock for me to chop against. She demonstrated with the first couple of pieces, me standing close in case she lost her balance. Then I took over. I stood the log up on the rock, tapped the ax into the end of it until it stuck, lifted the log and ax together, and brought them down.

Crack! What a sweet sound. The log split in half.

We made a proper fire pit nearer to the cabin by collecting rocks and arranging them in a circle. Mrs. Burt got me to set up kindling in a tepee shape over some twigs and dried leaves. After the flames got going, I added larger and larger pieces of wood and, before I knew it, I'd built my first bonfire. For supper we roasted hotdogs over it, on sticks, just like they do in books.

Artie danced around waving his in the air.

"Is that your sword?" Mrs. Burt asked.

"It's my magic wand."

"If it was a sword, you could knight us."

She explained that to become a knight the king laid his sword on you and pronounced you so. She used me as an example.

"I pronounce you Sir Curtis."

"I pronounce you Sir Mrs. Burt," Artie said, laying the greasy hotdog on her shoulder.

"Imagine that," she said. "Knighted with a wiener."

In their buns, even without the ketchup I forgot in the car, they tasted good. Better than microwaved.

After the fire had burned down to embers, Mrs. Burt put the kettle on for tea. She said the cabin was too dirty to sleep inside. We would spend the night under the stars. I went around cutting pine boughs to make mattresses. Then Artie and I unrolled our new sleeping bags.

"Bindlestiffs," said Mrs. Burt by the fire.

"What?"

"That's what we called bedrolls. Bindlestiffs. I don't know why."

We got comfy in our bindlestiffs. The boughs were lumpy, but every time I moved they gave off a woodsy smell, like air-freshener spray. Mrs. Burt slurped and burped. The fire made crinkling-paper sounds.

The night noises were new. The ones I was used to — sirens and traffic and people in the other apartments arguing or playing their stereos too loud — were far away.

Years ago, when I stayed with the Pennypack-ers, it had seemed like the wilderness because of all the trees, but there were still wide streets and two-car garages and telephone poles and strip malls.

There were none of those things here. We were in the wild.

Something rustled in the trees and Artie snug-gled close to me.

"A squirrel! A squirrel is coming!"

"Probably a mouse," said Mrs. Burt. "Squirrels go to bed the same time we do."

Then we heard a really creepy sound, like the craziest, loneliest person in the world calling out for help. Artie sat up with a gasp.

"Loon," said Mrs. Burt.

"Mom!" Artie cried.

"You bring that lotion down from the Chevy?" Mrs. Burt asked me.

I wriggled out of my bag and went and got it.

After Artie settled, I lay back and watched the light show of stars coming out. I'd never done that before. Somehow I had the idea that they switched on like streetlights. But as the pink faded from the sky, more and more stars crowded out the darkness. I fell asleep, and when I woke up in the middle of the night, there were even more of them. Stars sprayed out above me like frozen fireworks, a whole part of the sky so thick with them it looked white.

I didn't get it. In the city, where did the stars go?

THE NEXT DAY the sun woke me up earlier than I'd ever been up in my whole life. I didn't care because when I sat up and looked around, the lake was there. A whole lake with a sun and clouds floating in it, like the sky lying on the ground. It seemed like it was mine.

I made another fire and Mrs. Burt cooked us hash browns and sausages and eggs in a cast-iron pan, one of the few things we hadn't burned, because we couldn't. It was indestructible. The food tasted better than all her other breakfasts just because it was cooked over a real fire.

Then we got to work scrubbing out the cabin. I even had to get on the roof and be a chimney sweep, which meant I jammed a long stick down the stovepipe to clear out any bird or squirrel nests.

When we were done, Mrs. Burt said that it was going to be a very cozy place to live.

"You boys sure worked hard. I think you deserve a treat. I think you deserve a little fishing. What do you say?"

"Yeah!"

With the rods propped against the walker and Mrs. Burt settled on a rock, she prepared the tackle. We were after trout, she said. The lures she chose were silver with four orange beads. I thought they would make good earrings. If I ever got my ears pierced like Mr. Bryant, I'd wear lures.

Mrs. Burt handed us the rods. She used the walker to get up, but set it aside once she was standing where she wanted to be on the shore. She was much steadier on her feet now. I passed her my rod and she waved us to one side. We had to be very, very careful when we cast not to hook each other, or her. In fact, Artie wasn't allowed to cast, only to reel in.

She unlocked the reel, tipped the rod back over her shoulder, flung it straight. The lure winged out, then plopped into the water a long way away. Then she started reeling, slowly turning the handle, humming. As soon as we could see the lure in the water, she reeled faster.

"You don't want to get it snagged on the bottom." She cast a few more times, then passed the rod to me.

"Be careful you don't cross lines with us," she said. Then she and Artie and the thingie moved farther down the shore.

I unlocked the reel, drew back the rod, snapped it forward.

Wheee!!! The lure sailed out over the water and splashed down. I began to reel in, praying for a fish. I didn't know what I'd do if I caught a fish, but I wanted one. The reel *click-click-clicked*. My hopes got even higher. When I saw the lure sparkling under the water, I reeled faster, not even disappointed, just ready to cast and hope all over again.

But it turned out a big part of fishing is waiting, which is something little kids don't do well. Mrs. Burt had promised Artie a fish and now she had to get him to stay still for long enough that a fish would get interested in his hook. She started making up a story about King Arthur and the Knights of the Round Table. Her knights were more like lumberjacks. She was King Arthur's mulligan mixer, the only woman around. As a prank one of the logger knights stole her measuring cup and hid it in the forest. These knights were always pulling pranks, she said, like cutting the buttons off each other's Stanfields.

In the middle of the story, Artie's line jerked and the rod almost pulled right out of his hands.

"Hold on, Artie!" Mrs. Burt cried.

Behind him, her hands over his, she helped

him reel in. The tip of his rod bent over the water and suddenly the fish burst through the surface, flipping and twisting in the air.

Artie shrieked and ran back to the cabin.

"Give me a hand here, Curtis," Mrs. Burt called, trying to grab the slippery body dancing on the line.

I started to reel in. Then I felt a pull, too.

For something only ten inches long, that trout was strong. We played tug-of-war for a minute, fish pulling me, me pulling fish, Mrs. Burt yelling instructions and still trying to grab hold of Artie's fish. My heart thrashed as hard as the trout.

When it finally flipped into the air, I heard myself holler with joy.

"Grab it!" Mrs. Burt called. "Grab it, then come grab Artie's!"

In my hand the live fish squirmed. I picked up my rod and ran to Mrs. Burt. It took me a minute to grab hers, too.

There I was, both hands full of living fish, both of us laughing so hard I couldn't understand what Mrs. Burt wanted me to do, which was pass her fish to her while I held mine on the ground.

"Now grab that rock and give it a bash," she said.

I took the rock and I bashed the fish. Then I stopped laughing.

It lay on the ground, still now, silver and spotted, the hook piercing its lip, blood oozing from its gills. The wet eye looked up at me.

Mrs. Burt handed me the other fish and I killed it, too, before I had to think about it.

That was the one part of fishing I didn't like.

Afterward, Mrs. Burt showed me how to pull out the hooks with pliers and how to clean the fish and spill the guts into the lake. Fish guts were clean, she said. They were food for other fish. I cut the heads off, too, and wrapped the clean fish bodies in a damp cloth to keep them cool. Then I started fishing all over again.

As she headed with her contraption back up to the cabin where Artie was still hiding, Mrs. Burt said something really true.

"The hardest thing in the world, Curtis, is catching just one fish."

That night she got the woodstove fired up to cook our fish. I caught a lot of fish over the next few weeks — so many I lost count — but none ever tasted as good as those first two. Because when we caught them, and when I ate them, I actually forgot my mom was gone.

9

IN THE CABIN there was a kitchen sink and a hand pump that brought water from the lake, but there wasn't any real plumbing. The dirty dishwater just drained into a pipe that led to the trees instead of the lake. Mrs. Burt said we could pee wherever we wanted as long as it wasn't near or in the water. That was one of the best things about the cabin — peeing outside.

One of the worst was doing that other thing.

The morning after we got there, Mrs. Burt set up a little area off the road, far from the cabin where there was an old fallen log a few steps into the trees. We had to squat on the log, do our business over the other side, then scatter leaves around so the next person wouldn't have to see it.

It was horrible. Artie would say he didn't have to go even though he'd be dancing around trailing farts. Finally, really desperate, he'd admit it.

Then I'd have to take him to our "bathroom" and hold his hand the whole time, just like at home, even though he couldn't possibly be flushed down. I had to be there in case any squirrels came around.

"They'll bite my bum!"

"They won't," I said.

"They'll bite my pee-pee!"

"Just finish, okay?"

On our third day at the cabin, we went back to town. We had a ton of errands, like the supermarket and the bank, where Mrs. Burt must have taken out a lot more money to pay for everything. This time we filled the Bel Air with flour and oats and food that was dried or canned or bottled, because we didn't have a fridge. Seeds and tomato plants. At a sporting goods store we got air mattresses for the beds. Then we stopped at the hardware store for lumber and a hammer, tape measure and nails. And a level and some other things. Mrs. Burt said we were going to build a proper outhouse.

The man who strapped the lumber onto the roof of the Bel Air kept saying, "This is one beautiful car. Yep, she's a beaut."

"Thank you very much," Mrs. Burt replied, patting her cap, like he was complimenting her.

Next stop was the mall, where Mrs. Burt bought clothes for us. She even got me special boots for wood chopping — leather with laces halfway up my shins. While I was admiring my feet in the store mirror, she purposely slammed her contraption right down on my toe. It didn't hurt at all.

The last thing we did in town — the last thing I did — was try phoning Mom again. I had in mind all the things I wanted to tell her if she answered. Things I was dying to say even before I asked, "Where have you been?" or "Why did you leave me again?" I wanted to tell her that I could chop wood and build a fire. That I'd been swimming in a lake that was so clean we were drinking out of it. (Mrs. Burt boiled the water first, but it was still really clean.) That I'd caught a fish with my own fishing rod and eaten it.

After two rings she answered and, without even thinking, I opened my mouth to spill out all my news.

But it wasn't her. It was some other woman's voice.

"The number you have dialed is no longer in service. Please hang up and try your call again."

Mrs. Burt and Artie were waiting in the car. She asked me what was the matter.

"The phone's disconnected," I told her.

All she said was, "I guess we don't have much reason to come back to town."

⟋

WE FINALLY FOUND where the old outhouse had been but it was too overgrown to use. The new spot had to be away from the cabin, too, but not too far. And it had to have a view.

"Sometimes you'll want to just sit out there and think," Mrs. Burt told us. "For times like that, it's nice to have something to look at."

The three of us searched, Mrs. Burt whacking her thingie around, until we finally settled on a place that was higher than the cabin and on flat enough ground that the outhouse would sit straight.

Then I had to chop down some trees to clear the area and open up the view, which faced the lake. It took a long time but was fun, too, especially in steel-toed boots. I dragged the trees I'd cut down closer to the cabin so that later I could saw them into logs for firewood.

The hole came next. Digging, digging, digging. There were so many rocks and roots, I felt like I was digging all the way to the other side of the earth.

Finally, after a whole digging day, the pit came up to my chest. Mrs. Burt said it was deep enough, which was good news because my hands were all blistered and my back was so sore I could hardly straighten.

The next day at breakfast, Mrs. Burt showed me a little sketch she'd made of the outhouse with the measurements marked on it. It looked like a ticket booth without a door.

"Better get started," she said.

"Me? *I'm* going to build it?"

I'd never built anything in my life. But I'd also never done most of the things I was doing now, so I thought, Okay. I can.

Mrs. Burt and Artie were putting in a garden. She got Artie to dig the plot by telling him there was buried treasure, which was the coins she kept tossing down when he wasn't looking. While they were busy with that, I worked on the outhouse. Now and then Mrs. Burt barked instructions to me.

I measured and cut the lumber and nailed together the frames for the floor and the three walls, wasting hardly any nails once I got the hang of it. A frame is really just a rectangle of two-by-fours with a little triangle at each corner to make it stronger.

One at a time I carried the frames out to the hole. I laid the floor frame and nailed the plywood on, leaving an opening above the hole. I put up the wall frames and nailed them to the floor, then to each other. The bench was just some two-by-fours covered with plywood, except for the open rectangle in the middle where you sat. On the plywood roof I nailed some thick black stuff called tarpaper, then piled tree branches on.

It took two days to build and after I finished, the first thing I did was test the view. I sat there looking out, feeling tired and sore but also happy. I'd never really thought about the bathroom before because it was always there. Now I had made one with my own hands. And Mrs. Burt was right. It was much nicer to look out at a lake full of fish than at your own goofy reflection staring back at you in the mirror.

I went and got Artie and Mrs. Burt. She took a turn testing the view.

"This is a fine outhouse, Curtis," she said. "Solid. I look forward to using it for real. Climb up, Artie."

"No," Artie said. "There's no seat."

"We'll sandpaper her all smooth so you won't get any slivers in you," Mrs. Burt told him.

"He's afraid of falling down the hole," I

explained. When I said this, Artie turned red, like it only just occurred to him that this was impossible.

"I'm not! I want a seat so I don't get slivers!"

I looked at Mrs. Burt, wondering if she was prepared to drive all the way back to town just to buy a toilet seat that Artie would probably still be afraid of sitting on. So far she'd done everything Artie wanted. But if she did that, she would have to do something about all his fears, which was impossible. He was afraid of so much. She'd have to chase every squirrel out of the forest. She'd have to sweep away all the spider webs and pine cones. Artie said pine cones looked like spiky poo.

Mrs. Burt didn't offer to get a toilet seat. She smiled at me, tricky, tricky, showing all her brown teeth. She was smart. Really smart.

She said, "Artie? Remember how I told you about the quest for the holy measuring cup?"

He thought she was about to launch into another story.

"There was another thing they were looking for. Something even more important and more precious than that old cup."

"What?" Artie asked.

"A long, long time ago, in this very place, there was an outhouse, but nobody was around to use

it so it fell apart and all the boards rotted away.
But the toilet seat didn't rot. It's still around here
somewhere, probably half sunk into the ground
and overgrown with plants."

"Can we find it?" Artie asked.

"We're going to try. It's going to be *our* quest. In
the meantime, could you use the outhouse without the seat? Because I, for one, wouldn't want to
sit on any other."

Artie was so excited that he said yes. They set
off right away. An hour later they had to come
back empty-handed so Sir Mrs. Burt could cook
supper.

It gave me an hour to fish.

That night, after King Artie fell asleep, I sat by
the fire with Mrs. Burt and we laughed together about the Knights of the Round Toilet Seat.
She told me how brave King Artie had been, not
even shrieking when they came face to face with
wild pine cones. And Sir Mrs. Burt, who couldn't
maneuver her trusted steed, her contraption, her
thingie, in the forest, left it behind. She found a
walking stick instead. She felt pretty brave herself
hobbling around with just that.

"Is there really a toilet seat?" I asked.

"There used to be. It's got to be somewhere."

Mrs. Burt drank her tea and I watched the fire.

Even with the cabin cleaned and set up, we built a fire every night to keep the mosquitoes away. And for entertainment. Watching a fire is as good as TV. I don't know why.

Then Mrs. Burt asked me the question I hated most.

"Where's your father, Curtis?"

I shrugged and told her how he was just some guy my mom had known and that, except for me, she wished she'd never met him. Mrs. Burt shook her head.

"What?" I said. "We don't need him. Plenty of kids I know have dads and wish they didn't." I could have used Artic's father, Gerry, as an example. We sure didn't need him. Or Mr. Penny-packer, who was away working most of the time, but whenever he was home would just pick on Brandon and tell him how fat he was.

"You have your mother," Mrs. Burt said.

"That's right. We do." I felt myself turn red when I said it.

We hadn't had her for a long time.

"You don't have to get so defensive," Mrs. Burt said. "I'm just asking out of concern."

"You and Mr. Burt got divorced," I pointed out. "Your daughter didn't have a father around."

Mrs. Burt sat up straight like I'd poked her

with a stick, her tea mug held out so she wouldn't get sloshed.

"We did not! I was married to Mr. Burt for twenty-four years! Married to him till he died! Where'd you get that idea from?"

"I thought that was why you wouldn't come up here with him anymore."

"That's not why."

"You seem to love the place so much."

"I do!" she said. "Anyway. I was just curious about why you came away with me so easy when you hardly knew me. Why didn't you go across the street and tell the police about your mom?"

"No way," I said.

"Why not?"

So I told her about the Pennypackers and sharing a room with Brandon.

"He did this thing. He divided the room in half with a piece of string. I wasn't allowed on his side, but he could cross into mine any time he wanted. The door was on my side, so he had to. But the dresser was on his. When I got dressed in the morning, I would try not to step over the string, just reach across and get my clothes out of the drawer. Then he changed the rules so that reaching counted, too. When he caught me, he would move the string over."

Mrs. Burt said, "A string can't hurt you."

"I didn't know that. I was only six."

"What happened when he moved it?"

"My half got smaller. But if it ever reached the wall on my side of the room, I would cease to exist. That's what he said. *Cease to exist.* I believed him because he made my tooth fall out with his powers. He said he could make all my teeth fall out. Without teeth I wouldn't be able to eat."

And I told her how, when we left the house in the morning, as soon as we were out of sight of Mrs. Pennypacker smiling and waving from the front window, Brandon would go through my lunch and take everything he wanted, leaving me just the carrot sticks. At supper, Mrs. Pennypacker would practically beg me to eat. She would ask me what I liked and make it for me. But whatever she cooked made me gag because I couldn't be sure Brandon hadn't spat in it. I got thinner and Brandon got fatter. She worried about me, but she worried more about Brandon because he was her kid.

"I'd blast him one!" Mrs. Burt cried. "Imagine somebody doing something like that to Artie?" There was nothing she liked more than to cook for us and to watch us eat her cooking.

"Exactly," I said. It hurt, though, that she didn't

seem to feel bad for me, the kid it had really happened to.

"You did the right thing coming with me."

"I hope so," I said.

She looked at me across the fire. "When you
came to me that first time, Curtis? You were
hungry."

"Yes," I admitted. "This is way better, Mrs.
Burt."

"BOYS, I AM dispensing with this thingie. I am
standing on my own two feet." And she walked
across the cabin without her walker, keeping one
spotty hand held out in front of her, just in case.
Artie and I clapped.

After that the walker became Artie's toy. He
laid it on the ground and sat inside it. With a
board end left over from the outhouse as paddle,
he canoed for hours with Happy wired to a rail.
Or he draped it with the tablecloth to make his
own little cabin to live in with his china boy and
girl. He used it when he burped Mrs. Burt while
she washed the dishes, dragging the walker up behind her and standing on a rung.

She could burp all the way to the letter G now.

Artie's other favorite game was taxi. We would walk up to the Bel Air, and I would pretend to call from a secret taxi phone in a tree. Then Artie would drive me wherever I wanted to go. The fare was always the same. Four dollars plus tip. He would take me to the zoo, to the PNE, to the beach. But more and more I found it hard to think of going somewhere else. Because I was fine at the cabin — fishing, wood chopping, fishing, helping Mrs. Burt with her garden, fishing.

And swimming.

The first time we saw Mrs. Burt in what she called her "bathing costume," Artie and I laughed. She always dressed like a man in a knitted cap. But in her bathing suit she was like an elephant stuffed into a tutu. The rubber flowers on her cap quivered. All her rolls quivered. Her feet seemed a hundred years old with their lumps and bumps and thick elephant nails.

Giggling, we watched her limp toward the lake, arms held out, wings of jiggly upper arm flesh hanging down. She waded in up to her huge thighs, then plunged, making tidal waves slosh out on either side.

But then she changed. Mrs. Burt was practically crippled on her feet, but she was graceful in the water. She was a young person when she swam.

On shore, Artie and I watched her arms dip in rhythm and the rubber flowers turn left then right as she took her breaths. The water seemed to move aside for her as she plowed through it. We didn't giggle then.

After she had her swim, we got in the water with her. Artie wore a life jacket at all times and mostly just pulled himself along the lake bottom kicking his feet behind him. Or he brought the walker in and leapt off it. She was trying to teach him to put his head in, but he was afraid of getting water up his nose.

I was a better student. She helped me improve my technique with little suggestions like cupping my hands tighter so the water wouldn't flow through my fingers.

I asked how long it would take to swim across the lake.

"You think you can?" she asked.

I knew I could. I'd done so many incredible deeds lately I couldn't stop.

"It'll take about a half hour," she said. "You're going to have to practice every day."

"I will," I said.

Before we went to the cabin, I'd only ever swum in pools when they gave free lessons to inner-city kids. Lake swimming was different. There were no soggy Band-Aids floating around, nobody's hair getting tangled in your fingers. No stinky chlorine or screaming kids or shut-downs when a baby pooped.

You could open your eyes and see fish. See the long reaching arms of underwater trees. You could swim through whole forests. When you were tired, you could climb out and rest on a log. I liked to lie there in the sun and watch the drag-onflies zip against the blue like they were sewing on the sky.

10

WEEKS MUST HAVE passed because Mrs. Burt declared that we were as brown as mushrooms and at least three inches taller. I peeled back the band of my swimming trunks. From the waist up and the knee down I was the color of toast, but in between I was the same white as the homemade bread Mrs. Burt baked for us in the woodstove. For sure our hair was three inches longer.

"Time for haircuts," she announced.

We brought a chair out of the cabin and Mrs. Burt went first, popping a bowl on her head and handing me the scissors. "This is how I kept the fellows looking spruce when I cooked in the logging camp."

Spruce meant neat. She definitely did not look spruce when I was finished with her, but she didn't care. She just tucked what was left of her white hair up into her cap and told Artie to climb up

144

on the barber chair. She pushed the bowl down on his wild head and snipped around it so fast he didn't have time to squirm.

Then it was my turn. When she was through with us, the ground was covered with brown curls mixed with her white wisps. I was glad that there weren't any mirrors around. Well, there were a couple up in the Bel Air and a little one in Mrs. Burt's purse. Artie looked pretty funny so chances were that I did, too.

"Come with me, boys," she said then. "Let's find the growing tree."

We didn't know what she meant. All the trees were growing. The plants in her garden were growing. Everything was growing.

It took a while to find the tree she was searching for. When she found it, she showed us some thick, inch-long scars in the bark starting from about the level of my thigh. Every time Mrs. Burt and her family came to the cabin, they cut a notch at the height of Marianne.

"How tall is Marianne now?" Artie asked.

Mrs. Burt thought about it. "I have no idea."

"I want a notch," said Artie.

"And you shall have one, King Arthur," Mrs. Burt told him. She sent me to get the ax. Artie leaned up against the tree and I carefully scratched a line in the bark above his head. He stepped aside and I chopped out the notch.

"You, too, Curtis," Artie said.

I went around the tree. On the other side was another set of notches — a set that stopped around the same level Artie's notch had.

As soon as I saw that little ladder of scars, I understood everything. Why Mrs. Burt never came back here. Why she cried when she saw the place again. Why she was so in love with Artie, but me, not so much.

She had brought us to the tree on purpose, so she could tell us what had happened. She was ready now.

She led Artie around the tree so the three of us could see the notches that ended too soon.

"These are Clyde's," she said.

"Clyde who?" Artie asked.

"Clyde, my little boy . . ." She took a breath. "He died. It was a long time ago."

"How?"

"He drowned."

"Where?"

"In the lake."

"Our lake?"

"Yes. I wasn't watching carefully enough. But it won't happen to you because I'm always watching. Also, he was not as sensible a little boy like you are. He didn't have any fear. He would jump right in the water without making sure that his sister was there. You would never do something like that."

"No," said Artie. "I don't have a sister."

"You'll be fine."

"Did you cry?" Artie asked.

Mrs. Burt's eyes started blinking fast behind her glasses.

"I did. Quite a lot."

"Where is he now?" Artie asked.

"Clyde? He's in heaven for sure."

"Where is heaven?"

"Where is heaven? My goodness, the stuff you boys don't know! It's the most beautiful place. A place safe from all the trials of this world. There isn't any pain or unhappiness. There isn't any hunger. You eat anything you want whenever you want. You play all day long."

"Are we in heaven, Mrs. Burt?" Artie asked and Mrs. Burt, who had been struggling to hold back tears, laughed. Artie and I laughed, too, but only to keep her company. Inside, I felt so sad for her.

She took off her glasses and wiped them. "It does seem like heaven here, doesn't it?" Then, probably to stop him from asking more questions, she got me to fetch the Coca-Cola crate out of her bedroom and pry the lid off.

Inside were toys. Matchbox cars and books and an old stuffed bear that reeked and probably should have been burned but I wasn't going to suggest it.

Artie really was in heaven then.

A FEW DAYS later Mr. Munro came back across the lake. I was fishing when he paddled up. Artie and Mrs. Burt were off being Knights of the Round Toilet Seat. I didn't tell him that. I said they were out looking for something. After a couple of minutes of him just sitting there sucking his teeth behind his yellow moustache, I got nervous and reeled my line in.

"Any luck?" he asked.

I actually hadn't caught a fish in a while. In the beginning I'd caught one or two a day, but that seemed like a long time ago.

When I told him that, Mr. Munro said, "Lake's warmed up. Try deeper. It's colder." He had to bump the canoe right up next to me before I realized he was inviting me to get in.

Lying in the bottom were two huge dead, brown-and-black birds. I passed him my rod and he passed me the birds, which I had to hold by their scaly black ankles. Happy's plastic feet with their wires sticking out suddenly seemed cute.

"Leave them. So she knows who you absconded with."

I smiled. Mr. Munro and Mrs. Burt had the same funny way of talking. Mr. Munro probably knew what a bindlestiff was and a mulligan mixer, too.

I dumped the birds in front of the cabin and got in the canoe with Mr. Munro. There was a pretty strong smell coming off him, though it wasn't all bad. He smelled mostly like woodsmoke. I remembered to bring the life jacket. I always kept it nearby — not because I was worried about drowning, but because I knew it made Mrs. Burt happy to see how careful I was. Mr. Munro just threw it in the bottom of the canoe and handed me the second paddle.

Once we left the shore, I saw why the cabin was where it was. Almost everywhere else along the lake the trees grew right up to the water. I also realized why we often saw Mr. Munro's smoke from Mrs. Burt's cabin, but we couldn't actually see his place. It was tucked into a bay, looking like a bunch of little cabins jumbled together.

And I saw that the lake was in a place I'd always

heard about. The middle of nowhere. Mr. Munro was steering us right into the middle of it. The middle of the lake in the middle of nowhere. It was the most beautiful place I'd ever been.

When we got there, he motioned for me to cast my line and let the lure go deep. Then he started paddling again, very slowly, while my line trailed out behind. The peaceful wait started. Mr. Munro waited, too, sucking on his teeth. He probably wasn't used to talking, living all by himself. Or maybe he lived in the middle of nowhere because he hated to talk. The only sound was that crazy loon calling out and the water dripping off the paddle and the papery whir of dragonfly wings.

I don't know how long we'd been out there when he finally did say something. I was so surprised that I jumped in my seat.

"How's your mother?" he asked.

Before we absconded with Mrs. Burt, I hadn't really understood what a day was, even though I'd learned it in school. A day is the earth making a complete rotation, turning to face the sun, then turning away again. When you have electricity and streetlights, when you live mostly inside, it's easy to forget. You don't ever see the sky getting light at dawn, or the way shadows sneak around you through the day, or how slowly the sun sinks below the trees in the evening, pulling all its colors down with it. You forget that so much happens in a day. You forget that a day is a very long time.

One June morning my mom didn't come home. From then on, I began to count the days, just like they keep track of days you're away at school. But since coming to the cabin, I'd been so busy that I'd stopped. I'd completely lost track of how long she'd been gone.

When Mr. Munro asked about her, I felt terrible — worse when I realized how many complete rotations of the earth had happened without me even thinking about her.

But that wasn't what Mr. Munro meant. He was talking about Mrs. Burt's daughter, the Big Shot lawyer Marianne.

"She's fine," I said.

"I'm glad to hear it. She was a good girl. Your grandma was way too hard on her in my opinion, but I see they made up."

"I guess so," I said, just as my rod lurched.

Mr. Munro didn't speak again, not even when I reeled in my fish. He just leaned over and peered at the gasping, thrashing trout I'd landed in the bottom of the canoe. Then he showed me all the rotten teeth that made up his smile.

Mrs. Burt was hollering and waving her arms on shore as we paddled in.

"I caught one!" I told her when I stepped out. "I finally caught one again!"

"Did you see what Mr. Munro brought? Two grouse. We are going to have a feast tonight. You get out of that canoe, Spar. You're eating with us. Come on."

While they argued about it, I went and got the knife so I could clean the fish and take it into the cabin for Mrs. Burt to cook.

Mr. Munro agreed to stay, so Artie and I hung around inside the cabin even though it was hot with the stove roaring. Artie sat in the middle of the floor in his walker canoe. He couldn't stop staring at Mr. Munro with his big beard and the little flask he pulled out of his shirt pocket when Mrs. Burt plunked down the teapot.

"What's that?" he asked as Mr. Munro added a splash from the flask to his mug.

"Medicine," Mrs. Burt answered. "I was telling the boys that Joseph — that's Mr. Burt — was a high rigger. Right, Spar?"

"What's that?" Artie asked.

"The fella who scampers up the tree and tops and delimbs it. You know, chops off all the branches," she said.

Mr. Munro nodded.

"Mr. Munro worked with Mr. Burt back in the days I cooked in the camp. Tell them about my cooking, Spar."

"Not bad."

Mrs. Burt threw a tea towel at him, but it didn't get anywhere close.

"We're sure going to have a good supper tonight. These boys haven't ever had grouse."

"What's grouse?" Artie asked.

"Those birds Mr. Munro snared for us. Tell them about when the grizzly came into camp."

Mr. Munro said nothing.

"Spar. Tell them."

"Me?" He thought a moment, trying to recall. A drink straight from his flask helped. "When he got us all up the tree?"

"Yes," said Mrs. Burt, taking the lid off a pot and poking inside it.

"A bear came along and Joe got us all up a tree."

Mrs. Burt sighed. "This big old grizzly wanders into camp. Nowhere to go but up. Half the fellas were terrified of heights. That's something you probably wouldn't guess about loggers. Most of them are happier on the ground.

"In a matter of minutes, there's a big logger sitting up on every branch, swinging his boots, thumbing his nose at the biggest grizzly you ever seen."

"I remember now," said Mr. Munro.

"Tell them, then."

"Conk rot."

"The tree looked fine from the outside," Mrs. Burt explained, "but it was all rotten inside. With the weight of those boys sitting in it, the thing just keeled. Crash! Oh, the screaming. I tell you, that bear took off and it never came back."

"What if a grizzler comes here?" Artie asked with a wail.

Mr. Munro put together a few more words than usual.

"Don't worry, son. It's mostly blackies around here."

When supper was ready, we sat around the table in the cabin and Mrs. Burt said grace, which she normally didn't do with us. I think she was trying to make a good impression on Mr. Munro, who took a big swig out of his flask after the "Amen."

Grouse is like chicken, but better. The meat is browner and tastier. Mrs. Burt roasted them and made gravy and potatoes and steamed greens from the garden, which were the only thing she made that I didn't like. We had to eat it or we would get rickets, she said. For dessert there were baked apples swimming in custard.

"How'd you like that, Spar?" she asked afterward.

His beard was decorated like a Christmas tree with half of his dinner.

"Not bad," he said.

I made a fire for us to sit around outside. Mrs. Burt kept burping into her fist. Artie came over, but she didn't want to burp the alphabet with Mr. Munro there so she got him singing instead. "I've Heard That Song Before." "It's a Long, Long Way to Tipperary." "I Don't Get Around Much Anymore." Those were the old songs they sang while they wandered the forest on their quest for the round toilet seat.

Artie stood by the fire, hands clasped, warbling at the evening sky. Each time he finished a song, Mrs. Burt clapped and asked Mr. Munro if he wasn't the cutest kid he ever saw while Mr. Munro shook his little flask hard over his tea mug, like he shook the salt shaker at supper, trying to get the last drops out.

Then I took Artie off to bed. While I lay there waiting for him to fall asleep, I could hear Mrs. Burt talking at Mr. Munro. I didn't really listen until Mr. Munro said something.

"You always pick favorites, Mavis."

"What do you mean by that?"

"You didn't even cook his fish."

"You brought grouse. I'll cook it tomorrow."

"You didn't say nothing to him about it."

"He catches fish all the time."

Then she did something surprising. She started bragging about me and my outhouse and my wood chopping and swimming and how well I looked after my little brother.

"He's sharp," she said.

After Artie fell asleep, I went outside again. Mr. Munro looked up as I approached the fire.

"I hear you're going to swim across the lake."

"I might," I said, "if I get good enough."

Mr. Munro sank into his beard. Then he noticed something in it and ate it.

11

AN OUTHOUSE SHOULD be a good place to think. That's what Mrs. Burt said and, ever since Mr. Munro's visit, I started using it for that.

It actually didn't smell. We cleared the ashes out of the fire pit every day and left them in the outhouse in a box. Instead of flushing, you took a big scoop of ash with the tomato can and sprinkled it down the hole. Also, there was always a breeze off the lake.

I went there because of what Mr. Munro asked me in the canoe. I went to think about my mom. Usually I went when the Knights of the Round Toilet Seat were on their quest. Or, if I happened to be there anyway, I just sat a little longer. If I added up all the hours, I must have sat about a week.

What did I think about?

Where she was. What she was doing. If she was okay.

And I worried. What if she'd met another guy with the sleeves ripped off his T-shirt, like Gerry? What if that was what had happened?

Gerry had cast some kind of spell on her. She told me so herself. He had powers, like Brandon. Brandon had controlled me with his powers and Gerry had controlled Mom. He played songs for her on his guitar — songs about her, that he would write himself. She was flattered. It was hard looking after a little kid all on your own, especially when you were only twenty-one, and everybody else was out having fun. When Gerry drank, she felt she had to keep him company. If she didn't, he might stop playing songs for her. Then where would she be? Alone again in a crummy apartment, bored and poor.

She told me all this in the Pennypacker livingroom after Social Services started letting her visit me for an hour every Saturday.

"You weren't alone," I told her. "You had me."

"I know, I know." She put her face in her hands. "I'm so sorry. I made a terrible mistake. I want you back so badly."

Those were my outhouse thoughts. I usually went back to the cabin feeling pretty rotten.

Around that same time Artie started getting up in the night and going into Mrs. Burt's room to sleep with her. When I woke up in the morning, his sleeping bag would be crumpled beside mine, empty and cold.

"Why did you go to Mrs. Burt last night?" I asked him.

"I got scared."

"Of what?"

"A spider."

"Where's this spider? Show me." We searched the room but never found it. "Anyway," I said, "spiders are good. They can't hurt you."

Artie said, "I wouldn't be afraid of them if they didn't have so many legs!"

"So if they had six legs instead of eight they wouldn't bother you?"

"No."

"But you're scared of bugs, too. They only have six legs."

"I wouldn't be scared of them if they had four legs."

"Squirrels have four legs."

"If squirrels had two legs, I'd like them better."

"So you're not afraid of people?"

"No. Except for that man at the motel. And Brandon Pennypacker."

About a week after Mr. Munro's visit, Sir Mrs. Burt and King Arthur came back to the cabin very excited. The blueberries were ripe.

"Boys, I'm going to make you the best jam you ever tasted," Mrs. Burt said. Artie cheered because he'd long ago licked clean the little jam packets that Mrs. Burt had loaded in her purse on our road trip. "And the best pie you ever tasted," she went on. "The best flapjacks you ever tasted."

She took three old cans and got me to punch two holes in each of them. Then she threaded a string through the holes to make a sort of necklace. With the cans bumping around our necks, and a bucket in Mrs. Burt's hand, we headed out.

We were supposed to drop the berries into the can around our necks until it was full, then empty it into the bucket and start picking all over again. But the wild blueberries were so good. They were smaller than the ones you get in the store and twice as sweet. Artie picked them straight into his mouth. Once in a while I'd hear the *ping* of one landing in his can, probably by accident.

Mrs. Burt had both hands going so fast that she emptied her can twice into the bucket and moved on to the next bush before I emptied mine once.

Now that I was spending all that time in the

outhouse thinking about Mom, I wanted to talk about her to Artie, but not in front of Mrs. Burt. It had been ages since Artie had even mentioned Mom. We hadn't used the Economizer Extra-Strength Hand and Body Lotion since our first night at the cabin. So when Mrs. Burt got a little farther up the path, out of earshot, I asked him what he missed most about Mom now.

He looked at me, his face purple with berry juice. "Nothing."

I remembered exactly how I felt when I was his age and separated from my mother. It was the worst thing that ever happened to me.

"You do miss her, Artie. I know you do."

"I don't!" He stamped his foot on the ground. I was shocked, but also afraid of starting a fit so I didn't push it.

And then I realized what I'd been doing wrong. Because I worried about making Artie cry, I didn't talk to him about Mom.

Now I said, "Well, *I* miss Mom. I miss how she smells. I miss when she phones from school to say goodnight. I miss spinning around while she's on the phone and falling on the floor and her getting all worried when she hears the thump. I miss doing homework with her. The way she holds her pencil in her teeth."

I snuck a look at him. He was pretending not to hear.

"What about you?" I asked.

"I don't remember."

"I think you do. I think you remember sucking her hair to get to sleep. I think you remember peeking under her eye mask and growling."

Artie swung around with a horrible cannibal face.

"Mom's no good!" he screeched.

I froze. The berry I'd just picked fell to the ground. From the corner of my eye, I saw my hand lift high in the air. I wondered what it was going to do.

Hit him? Yes. I was about to hit my brother for what he'd just said about our mother.

I'd never hit a person in my life.

Then I heard a snort from Mrs. Burt. The weird thing was, she seemed to be coming back in the opposite direction from the one she'd left in. Coming just in time to see the slap that was itching at the end of my hand.

When she snorted a second time, I looked past Artie.

It wasn't Mrs. Burt. A bear was lumbering toward us, its snout twitching in the air.

Everything went quiet. So quiet I could hear Mrs. Burt humming "I've Heard That Song

Before" from where she was picking berries way up the path in the other direction. I think I even heard her berries plinking in the can.

The bear's head thrashed from side to side and he reared up on his hind legs, enormous and black. He made an awful bear sound, not a snort at all, and Artie spun around. He didn't seem surprised by the bear towering over him.

Then an angry chirring sounded.

"Watch out!" Artie screamed at the bear. "There's a squirrel behind you!"

The bear spooked. It crashed to the ground and charged right past us, toward where Mrs. Burt was picking. A moment later we heard a scream, then a lot of noise, like trees ripping out by the roots. Mrs. Burt appeared, not quite running, puffing, her hand on her chest, the tin can swinging round her neck, blueberries flying everywhere.

By then Artie had collapsed on the path completely hysterical over the squirrel.

"Get the lotion!" Mrs. Burt roared, and without even thinking, I ran back to the cabin.

I couldn't find it. It wasn't in our room. I checked by the sink and on the shelves. The last place I looked was in Mrs. Burt's room.

That's where I found it, on her dresser. As I ran back, I noticed how light the bottle was.

THE PIE SIR Mrs. Burt baked that night was to celebrate King Artie's wondrous deed, how he drove away the fearsome bear *and* the fearsome squirrel.

"Weren't you frightened of that terrible bear?" Mrs. Burt asked him.

"No," said Artie, shoveling in the pie. "It only had two legs."

"I was terrified. I thought it had already killed you boys. I thought I'd find you eaten up on the path. What's the matter, Curtis? Don't you like the pie?"

I was poking at it with my fork.

"Not bad," I said, and she laughed, thinking I was imitating Mr. Munro.

Actually, it was the best pie I ever tasted, but I was too mad to tell her.

That night I didn't sit out and watch the fire with Mrs. Burt like I usually did. I got Artie to sleep and I stayed with him, listening for the owl that sometimes roosted close to the cabin. It sounded like somebody blowing over the mouth of a bottle.

When it was time to get ready for bed, Mrs. Burt shuffled inside, lit the kerosene lamp, brushed her teeth at the sink. I heard her slow steps carry her to her bedroom and the sounds she made as she undressed and put on her nightie.

Shuffle, shuffle. She came and stood in our doorway with the lamp, lifted it and shone it around the room. She was looking for the lotion. I sat up in my sleeping bag and rubbed my eyes, pretending that she had woken me with the light.

"What?" I asked.

"Nothing," she said, shining the lamp one more time at the dresser where the bottle of lotion used to be before she took it. "Go back to sleep."

I lay down again, smiling and feeling with my feet for the bottle at the bottom of my sleeping bag.

THE NEXT DAY I thought she would come right out and ask me where the lotion had got to. But she didn't. She didn't have to because Artie got up in the night and went to her anyway. She had been rubbing herself with that lotion to lure him away. Now that she had him trained, she didn't need it anymore.

I felt sorry for Mrs. Burt because she lost her little boy all those years ago. Now she was here with Artie and she wanted to give him all the love she couldn't give her own son. Even though I didn't like what she was doing, I understood.

But I was disappointed in Artie. When I stayed with the Pennypackers, whenever Mrs. Pennypacker tried to hug and kiss me, I would make myself as stiff as a piece of wood. I would turn my head to the side so her kisses could never reach me. All my kisses were for my mother, no matter what she'd done.

Artie had given up too easily on our mom.

That afternoon I asked Mrs. Burt again when I could swim across the lake. She asked if I thought I was ready, if I was strong enough. I told her yes.

"Show me then," she said, plunging forward.

We started to swim side by side, away from the shore where Artie was in the water with the walker, pretending it was a canoe. I turned my head to take a breath and saw Mrs. Burt right beside me. We were swimming neck-and-neck. And because we were so close, I felt spurred on to swim harder, to race her. I fluttered my feet and drove my arms into the lake, cupping the water and throwing it behind me the way she had shown me, so I would be faster.

Which I was, I saw, when I finally noticed that I was swimming alone. I stopped and looked around and saw Mrs. Burt's turquoise bathing cap bobbing far behind me and Artie on shore so small I could have squashed him between my thumb and finger.

That was when I realized I was floating in the middle of the lake in the middle of nowhere. There was nothing under my treading feet but a terrible black bottomlessness.

I felt so small. I felt like a little kid who'd lost his mother, who was losing his little brother, too. I panicked and started to flail, then sink. I swallowed water, coughed it up. I went under.

I was drowning.

Then Mrs. Burt's big wobbly arm reached out and flipped me on my back and started to tow me in.

SHE WOULDN'T SPEAK to me after that, she was so mad. She stayed in the cabin the rest of the afternoon smashing pans around, jamming sticks of wood into the stove, slamming the cast-iron door. Artie was so terrified he hid in our room. I went and sat in the outhouse and thought about Mom until Mrs. Burt called us to supper.

She had cooked so much food — biscuits, split

pea soup, potato hash with tinned meat, sliced to-
matoes from the garden, blueberry cobbler — all
of it crowding out the table. But because it had
been cooked in anger, it didn't taste as good. Also,
we weren't hungry. Neither was she. She drank
her tea and glared at us miserably lifting our forks
to our faces.

"What?" she snapped.

We hung our heads and chewed and, when we
had choked down all we could, I got up to clear
the table.

"That's it?" said Mrs. Burt.

"I'm not very hungry," I said.

"Not hungry? I thought you'd be starving after
that great big swim you had."

I knew I had to apologize.

"I'm sorry, Mrs. Burt. I'm sorry for swimming
ahead. It was stupid. I know I scared you. I scared
myself, too. I won't do it again."

She slammed her mug down. "Your little
brother was all alone in the water! What if something happened to him? Who was I supposed to
go to? Who was I supposed to choose?"

At the sound of her raised voice, Artie started
to cry. I looked at her, surprised she wouldn't au-
tomatically have chosen Artie. Then Artie's crying
registered and her expression softened.

"Get the lotion," she said to me.

"No."

"Pardon me?"

"I'm saving it for when we really need it. It's okay if he cries sometimes."

I guess that was the first time I said no to her because she looked shocked. A grunt escaped her. It sounded like the bear the day before. And something else. It reminded me of that time before we knew her, when Mom and Artie and I walked by her house. She grunted then, too, as we went by, like she disapproved of us.

She got up from the table, grabbed one of the pans, stomped over to the kitchen and began scraping food into the garbage. She'd never thrown out food before. Usually she made something else with the leftovers the next day — something just as good, or better.

"Mrs. Burt," I said. "What are you doing?"

"You don't like it."

Artie cried out, "We like it! We'll eat it tomorrow!"

"No. You don't like it. You probably prefer the kind of muck you used to eat."

"No!" Artie wailed. "*She* cooked terrible! I like what *you* cook!" And he dragged the barely touched cobbler dish over and began to spoon it into his mouth.

Muck.

I said, "Our mom's not as good a cook as you are, Mrs. Burt, that's for sure. But it wasn't muck."

"It *was* muck," Artie said, still stuffing himself. "She's a no-good cook!"

People are no good. Mom's no good. It sounded familiar now.

"Mrs. Burt? Have you been saying mean things about our mom to Artie?" I said.

"No, I haven't!" But she looked so flustered that I knew she had.

"You're always saying everything's so terrible now, not like in your day," I said. "That nobody has any pride."

"It's true!"

"It isn't! I have pride. Enough to ask you to stop turning Artie against our mom."

"I did not!" Mrs. Burt said, and again her guilty look said something else. "I was just trying to help him get over it."

"Get over what?"

Mrs. Burt, all bristled up until that moment, shrank down now to her normal unangry size. She shook her knitted cap.

"Oh, Curtis."

"She's coming back," I said.

"She's not."

"I'm ten out of ten positive she is!"

This was a lie. I was thinking more around a three by then.

Mrs. Burt said, her voice soft, "You don't believe that. You never believed it. If you did you wouldn't have come away with me. You would have done more to find her."

"What would I have done?" I asked.

"You would have . . . checked the hospitals." She turned very red when she said this and so did I because I'd never thought of it. If Mom was in the hospital, somebody would have told us.

I turned and ran out of the cabin. I kept on running up the road. I didn't know where I was running. If anything, it was away, away from what she had just said. Because I *did* doubt Mom was coming back. Why else was I running? As for the hospital, I put that completely out of my mind.

She couldn't be dead. She couldn't.

I tore into the trees. Branches whipped my face and ferns sliced my shins. I stumbled and crashed to my knees, panting hard. I had no idea where I was.

This was how Artie felt all the time. I was so impatient with him for being such a scaredy, but now I felt it, too.

I struggled to my feet and stared around me, completely lost.

Everywhere, trees. Just trees.

I had to find the lake. If I found the lake, I could walk around it. Even if I walked in the wrong direction, eventually I'd find my way back to the cabin.

I bushwhacked. A great whooshing sound exploded behind me, a bomb of feathers. I screamed and covered my head. Then I threw up all the supper I hadn't wanted to eat.

I counted my steps. One, two, three. When I did that, I stopped panicking. And as soon as I stopped panicking a glimmer appeared beyond the trees. One, two, three. One, two, three.

Finally I reached the shore all tangled with reeds, sat down and cried. But not for long, because it was starting to get dark. The days were shorter now. Summer was coming to an end.

I kept walking.

One, two, three. One, two, three. One, two, three.

The next time I stopped was on a mossy patch of ground. I badly needed to see things in a different way so I put my head on the ground and — one, two, three — kicked my legs up against a tree.

I missed my mom. I loved her.

On a scale of one to ten, how would I rate the chance of her coming back? Of her being a good mother?

Upside down, I clung to the tree, but when I looked out at the lake I saw a different number, one that was the same no matter which way you looked at it. A number was half sunk in the shallow water near the shore, among the stones and reeds.

On a scale of one to ten? Was she ever coming back?

A zero.

A toilet seat.

12

AFTER I FISHED the toilet seat out of the water, everything changed. All the way back to the cabin the trees sort of parted and I knew the way. Mrs. Burt and Artie were huddled by the fire, but they jumped up as soon as they saw me staggering toward them. The scratches on my face stung and my legs and arms were muddy and bleeding. In my outstretched hands was the toilet seat.

When they saw it, they whooped for joy. Artie started jumping around me, hugging me and saying, "You really are Sir Curtis, Curtis! You really are a hero!"

Mrs. Burt heated water on the stove to wash all my cuts and scratches. She bandaged the worst ones, then made a special tea and fed it to me with a spoon while she sang all her old songs for me. I fell asleep and didn't wake up until the middle of the next day.

When I did finally get up, I felt so light, like I had lost a hundred pounds overnight. It was the weight of all that worry finally lifting off. I wasn't waiting for Mom anymore. I wasn't wondering where she was. I was just living, like I had been before she went away.

Mrs. Burt polished up the toilet seat for a special ceremony.

With towels as capes and clover chains as crowns, we marched in a procession to the outhouse. Artie led us, carrying the toilet seat on a pillow.

"Brave King Arthur," Mrs. Burt said in a deep pretend voice, "we have succeeded in our noble quest. After thirty long years your most worthy knight, Brave Sir Curtis of the Round Toilet Seat, has returned this treasure to the royal outhouse. Your throne is now intact."

Then we cheered and Mrs. Burt took from the folds of her cape a special treat she had been saving — two bottles of orange pop. We poured a little down the hole of the outhouse to christen it. Then we drank the rest.

With the seat, the outhouse was much more comfortable than before, but I didn't go there anymore except when I had to. Whenever I thought of Mom I pushed her out of my head.

All her promises had been lies. I knew that now.

She was somewhere with some new guy, listening to his dumb songs. She had probably ripped the sleeves off her T-shirts, too.

Mrs. Burt and I finally swam across the lake together. Artie promised to stay in the cabin. He stayed inside with his life jacket on and played with Clyde's Matchbox cars and Smelly Bear and Happy and the china boy and girl.

According to Mrs. Burt's watch, it took twenty-four minutes to swim across and thirty-three minutes to swim back because we were tired. From the other side we could see Mr. Munro's place.

The feeling I had crawling back on shore after the swim was total exhaustion. Also total satisfaction. I flopped onto my back and watched a honking V of Canada geese fly over, breaking up the blue.

"Right on time," said Mrs. Burt, who sat beside me in her dripping tutu. "There's a nip in the air in the mornings. Do you feel it, Curtis? Fall comes fast up north."

What were we going to do? When she invited us to the cabin, she called it a holiday. I never wondered how long the holiday would be. By now Nelson would have rented our apartment to somebody else. The police would have forgotten all about us.

I told this to Mrs. Burt that night around the fire.

I said, "We should probably go back." Artie was supposed to start grade one. He had to learn to read.

"Why can't I teach him? It can't be that hard. As for you, you've learned more this summer than you ever did in all your years doing the three Rs."

"What are the three Rs?"

"Reading, Writing, Rithmetic."

That made me wonder if she was the best person to teach Artie.

She read my mind and said to Artie, "Go and get one of those books of Clyde's out of the box." He came back with exactly the one she needed, an alphabet book.

"What's this letter, Artie?" she asked.

"I don't know," Artie said.

"It's A. Say A."

"A," Artie said.

"Give me your finger." He did and she took it and traced the letter for him, saying, "A," again. "Now pat my back."

He scampered behind her. He loved making her burp.

"A," she burped.

Artie giggled like it was the first time he had heard her do it.

"What's this letter?" she asked, pointing in the book.

"A!" Artie laughed.

Mrs. Burt looked at me in triumph.

"Do B now!" Artie screamed.

He is probably the only kid in history who learned his letters by the burping method.

And so I agreed we'd stay on a little longer and that Mrs. Burt would take charge of Artie's lessons. As for me, I hiked up to the Bel Air and brought down the pillowcase of schoolwork that I hadn't even looked at once.

The beginning of the school year was mostly review anyway. I could read over last year's work.

SOMETIMES ARTIE SLEPT with me, sometimes he slept with Mrs. Burt. It didn't hurt my feelings anymore when I woke in the morning and saw his sleeping bag at the bottom of the bed like an empty cocoon. It just meant he was in the next room with Mrs. Burt, not that he was any less of a brother to me. But the mornings were chilly now, so I liked it better when Artie was there. Because it was warmer.

We woke up whenever we felt like it. Artie was

almost always first. But one morning he just lay there working something in his mouth, a funny expression on his face.

"Are you sick?" I asked.

"I don't know."

"Do you feel sick?"

"No, but there's a pill in my mouth." He stuck out his tongue. Sitting there on the pink cushion of it was his tooth.

A memory came back. Not Brandon's hand feeling under my pillow for the dollar, but Mom waddling into the Pennypackers' living-room behind her big stomach. She never missed a visit even though it took her three buses to get there. But it seemed like she'd grown huge in just a week.

I pointed at the bulge and asked, "What's that?"

She laughed. "This is your brother who you're going to meet in a few weeks."

I started to cry then. I probably pitched a fit. Mrs. Pennypacker came running. When she saw I was all right, that Mom was hugging me, she walked backward out of the room again. Brandon was gaping in the doorway and she made him leave, too.

I was crying because I knew then I would have to live with the Pennypackers for the rest of my life. The rest of my short life, because the string in the bedroom was barely a hand space from the wall. This was probably the last time I would see my mother before the string touched the wall and I ceased to exist. She would have another little boy in a few weeks. She didn't need me anymore.

"No, Curtis," she said. "This little baby is going to help me get you back."

"How?"

"He's going to be born and I'm going to look after him. I'm going to take better care of him than any mother ever did. And when they see what a good job I'm doing, when they see how much I love this little baby, they'll know I'm a good mother and they'll let me bring you home."

Then she took my hand and pressed it to her hard belly, the way she ended every visit. She pressed her other hand to my heart. I put my hand over hers. Our foreheads touched.

"I promise," she said.

This time I could feel Artie kicking to get out.

That's exactly what happened. Artie was born and she looked after him so well that every Saturday afternoon he was bigger and his little hand clutched my finger harder and he cried louder and nursed longer. So one of those Saturdays I said goodbye to the Pennypackers and the three of us went home.

"Hold still," I said to Artie. Very carefully, I lifted the tooth off his tongue. "Go and ask Mrs. Burt for her mirror. There's a nice space left in your mouth."

Off he scampered. In a second I was out of the bed, too, and clawing through the drawers until I found Mom's wallet. I opened it and there she was, looking at me from the community college I.D. card.

She wasn't smiling. She was just looking straight ahead, but her eyes seemed to be saying something to me now as I put Artie's tooth in the change compartment and zipped it up.

What were they saying?

They were asking for Artie's tooth.

I knew Mrs. Burt would want it. She would want it so Artie could put it under his pillow for the tooth fairy.

"How could you lose it?" she snapped at me. "You only had it for a minute!"

"I dropped it."

We unzipped our sleeping bags and shook them. When the bottle of lotion fell out of mine, Mrs. Burt gave me a look. We moved the bed away from the wall so she could sweep around it with the broom. Artie pitched a fit.

"Good thing we found the lotion," she said, glaring at me again.

In the end we used a substitute tooth, a pebble the same size. Artie got his dollar but Mrs. Burt still grumbled under her breath.

I TRIED TO be honest with her. I approached her at a good time, while she was cooking, and said, "Mrs. Burt, I have an idea."

"What?"

"I think we should go together to Social Services and say Artie and I want to live with you."

She was bent over stirring batter for johnny-cake, but now she jerked up straight.

"You're living with me now. Why should Social Services have to know?"

"I want to go back to the city."

She swung around so fast a big glob of batter flew off the spoon and landed halfway across the room.

"They'll never let you stay with a crippled old lady like me!"

"We've been staying with you all this time and you've looked after us really well."

Her eyes bulged behind her glasses. "You can't tell anybody that!"

"Why not?"

"I didn't have permission. I'll be in big trouble. Then my daughter'll sell me out and put me in a home."

"Mrs. Burt," I said, trying to calm her down. "Before we came away with you, I was afraid of going to Social Services. I thought they'd split up me and Artie and we wouldn't have any choice. But now that I swam all the way across the lake with you and came face to face with a bear? Now that I found the toilet seat? Convincing them to keep us together is going to be a snap compared to that."

Mrs. Burt shrieked, "They aren't going to give a hoot about that old toilet seat!" At the sound of her raised voice, Artie came tearing inside the cabin and ran to her.

"If we go back," she continued, "they are going to take you away for sure! They'll put me in a home and they'll split you up! They'll put you with those people again! The Pennywhatsits. You already know them so they'll think they're doing you a favor sending you back."

"I don't want to go with Brandon!" Artie wailed.

"Mrs. Burt," I said.

"No! No! No! No!"

AFTER SUPPER WE always sat together at the table for our lessons. I looked through my notes from last year. One section in my binder was called "Personhood." *Treat others with respect*, I had written. *Respect = not only what you say but how you say it. Be tolerant. Be compassionate. Exercise your extraordinary reasoning abilities at all times. That means: THINK ABOUT IT!!!!*

At the same time I was reading, I watched Mrs. Burt teaching Artie, Artie struggling to remember the sound each letter made. She took a slurp of tea. She loved her tea.

I got up for a knife to sharpen my pencil. At the same time, I took a peek in the tea canister. About a quarter full. The provisions were stored under the counter. There were cans and bags and bins of things — more of some, less of others. There was still a lot of oatmeal, for example. I lifted the lid off the big box that was labeled 3000 TEA BAGS. It was hard to say, but there might have been a few hundred cups to go.

That is, until I reached inside and grabbed about twenty bags and stuffed them in the hotdog pocket of my pants.

I went over to the woodstove and lifted a burner off with the handle. As I whittled my pencil to a sharper point, I let the shavings fall into the stove. Now and then I took a quick glance over my shoulder to make sure Mrs. Burt wasn't watching. Then I dropped a tea bag in. It smelled kind of funny, but she didn't notice.

I did that for a few days. Every time I went inside the cabin I burned a tea bag. I was going in and out a lot to get boiled water from the kettle to drink. Because you work up a thirst chopping wood and scouting trees to chop. We were burning more wood and, though Mrs. Burt didn't know it, we were burning a lot of tea bags, too.

When we ran out, we would have to go to town and buy some more.

What was I planning to do when we got to town? I wasn't sure. Maybe a police officer would wander into the supermarket and I'd just take him aside and explain the situation. I'd say that we'd been at our neighbor's cabin in the middle of nowhere but now I wanted to go home and find my missing mother so I could give her my brother's tooth. Even if she didn't want us back, it belonged to her. And if the officer asked me why, I'd say because it went with the other one she already had. Or used to have. The one that was taped inside a stranger's bathroom cupboard now.

Actually, I tried not to think about what I would do in town, because in every case the police officer burst out laughing and walked away shaking his head.

The mistake I made was talking too often about going to town. I slapped my binder closed and said, "I already know all this stuff, Mrs. Burt. We need to *go to town* so that I can get some new books."

Mrs. Burt took the binder from me and opened it at random.

"What's the square root of sixty-four?"

"Square root? Is that like finding the area of a square?"

She slid it back to me and tapped her finger on the question I'd got wrong.

A few minutes later, she brought over cookies and milk for a snack. Our milk was powdered.

I said, "I'd do anything for a glass of real milk. Or ice cream. Can we *go to town* for ice cream?"

She squinted at me through her glasses. Then she belched.

13

THE CABIN SMELLED of fresh baking when I woke up. Artie got up first and came back to bed with a blueberry scone. Everything seemed normal except for how quiet it was in the cabin without Mrs. Burt's humming filling it up.

I hoped she was in the outhouse, but then too much time passed and I knew she was gone. Still, I had to torture myself by getting Artie dressed and walking all the way up the road to see the four flat spots of yellow grass where the Bel Air had been parked for two months.

Artie thought we were going to play taxi. He was mad that I'd made him walk all that way for nothing. I sank down on the ground and put my head on my knees.

"Where's the car?" he asked.

"Mrs. Burt went to town."

"Why didn't she take us?"

We could reach the highway by following the road, but then what? Hitchhike? I'd seen those movies at school. Getting into a car with a stranger was about the same as asking to be murdered. Maybe I would have taken a chance, but not with Artie. I sure couldn't get him to walk all the way to town. But I couldn't leave him behind, either.

I was scared of Mrs. Burt now.

"She's thinks we're going to run away," I said.

"I'm not going to run away! I love Mrs. Burt!"

She had powers, too. She had cast a spell on Artie and turned him against our mom so he didn't believe in her anymore. She had made him love her instead.

"Come on," I said, getting to my feet. "Let's go back."

"I'm tired."

"I'll carry you." I squatted so he could climb onto my back. Then I staggered down the overgrown road, my little brother on my back, his hands too tight around my neck, singing at the top of his voice, "It seems to me I've heard that song before . . . I know it well, that melody . . ."

When we got back to the cabin, I left him and went and sat in the outhouse on the comfortable seat. I didn't think about my mom or anything. I just stared at the finger of smoke that pointed up from Mr. Munro's cabin.

I remembered the afternoon he took me fishing. If only we had a canoe, I could paddle over there and ask him to help us. Maybe I could build a boat. No, a raft. I'd built an outhouse. Maybe I could secretly build a raft.

From the middle of the lake the loon let go its crazy, lonely cry. The first time we heard it, the hair lifted on my arms and the back of my neck, but I was used to it now.

Mrs. Burt was like that loon. When we met her, she'd been a little crazy with loneliness. That was why she didn't want to go back to the city, I thought.

MRS. BURT HOBBLED into the cabin in the early afternoon with two things in her arms: another 3,000 tea bags and a carton of chocolate ice cream.

Artie ran to her. "Why didn't you take us? Why?"

"You boys were sleeping so peacefully I thought I'd just slip out."

When she handed me the ice cream, I pretended to be excited about it. I pretended not to mind that she'd gone to town without us.

"Ice cream!"

Then I did a stupid thing. I hugged her. I'd never done that before. She drew back with her eyes all narrow, and I realized that she had been expecting trouble from me.

"Thanks for remembering," I said, turning very red.

"Of course I remembered. I remembered the milk, too," she said with a sniff. "It's in the car. All I want is for you boys to be happy, Curtis. That's all I want in the whole world."

Artie and I ate the entire carton of ice cream for lunch. We had to before it melted. Then I walked up to the Bel Air and unloaded it.

Food. So much food. Tubs of shortening, bags of powdered eggs, sacks of onions and potatoes. There was more fresh food, too, but it was the canned and dried stuff that worried me. Trip after trip, I lugged it down. Then, when I looked in the bags from the department store and saw winter coats and mitts, I almost died. In another bag there were boots.

She planned on staying in the cabin for the winter. How? There was only the woodstove to heat and cook with. I would never be able to chop enough wood. And what about water? The lake would be frozen. We'd have to drink melted snow.

I brought all the bags down to the cabin and acted like I hadn't seen what was inside them. Mrs. Burt was busy organizing everything.

"Look what I got you boys! Look!" She rooted through a bag and pulled out a matching pair of long underwear. "Stanfields!" she cried.

They were a gray wool that itched your eyes just to look at them, one-piece with buttons up the front and a "trap door" in the back. Mrs. Burt showed us how the trap opened and closed, fixed at the corners with buttons. Artie put his on right away, as happy as a logger.

I'd get in Mrs. Burt's tutu before I got in those Stanfields. That's what I told myself.

I CAUGHT A bad cold. It was as though the ice cream had given it to me. I must have had a fever, too, because I thrashed around so much in my sleeping bag.

Sometime in the night I woke and saw Mrs. Burt snooping through the dresser. She took out Mom's wallet and emptied the change compartment into her hand.

"No!" I shouted.

Too late. She'd found Artie's tooth. She held it up and smiled. Then she swallowed it.

But it was just a bad dream. When I really woke up, I got out of bed and checked the wallet. The tooth was there.

I stayed in bed the next day. The day after that Mrs. Burt fed me a huge logger-style breakfast with the fresh eggs that she'd brought from town. I could tell she was worried. She watched me closely as I ate and felt my forehead several times. Worried about me, I thought. But after I finished eating and stood to take the dishes to the sink, she excused me.

"I'll do that, Curtis. You get started on the wood."

Dressed in my new wool socks and my new jeans and my trusty steel-toed boots, I left the cabin with my headache and my stuffed nose. I felt tired, but managed to scuff around in the woods until I found a good log. Dead, but not so dead that it was rotten. That was the kind of tree that made the best firewood. I started to saw it into choppable lengths but never finished the job because I suddenly felt dizzy. I had to go back in the cabin and lie down.

"You just rest up," Mrs. Burt said. "Don't push yourself."

Later, I heard her outside trying to chop the wood herself.

"Blast it, blast it, blast it," she kept muttering, before she gave up.

After lunch, she and Artie set out to gather sticks and branches.

"This will be our new quest," I heard her say to him.

Over the next few days, I'd wake feeling okay, eat a good breakfast, saw a couple of logs, carry them down and split them. Then I'd feel too tired to go on. All I wanted to do was lie by the stove. I took the air mattress off the bed and carried it out of our room and flopped down for the rest of the day. Mrs. Burt encouraged me to get up, to get moving. She'd bought me all kinds of books in town — science books that explained the stars, books about nature, adventure novels by Jack London that she said I'd love.

"Here," she said. "I got you one about the King Arthur legend."

I took it from her and put it under my head. The cover felt so cool under my hot cheek.

I wasn't faking it. I felt so tired it didn't even occur to me to pretend. But one morning Mrs. Burt stood over me with her hands on her thick waist and her glasses sliding down her nose.

"You're not on strike, are you, Curtis?"

I blinked up at her. "What do you mean?"

"Are you really sick or are you doing this on purpose?"

I was sick with hopelessness. I'd been lying by the stove because it seemed there was nothing else I could do. I couldn't change her mind about going back and I couldn't get us out except by leaving alone and risking that Mrs. Burt would abscond with Artie. Now she had told me exactly what I had to do to escape. I was already doing it.

Nothing.

"MAYBE I SHOULD take you to the doctor."

I sat up too fast on the air mattress. I coughed when I hadn't been coughing before.

"Now?" I asked.

Mrs. Burt shuffled over to a chair and sank down on it.

"Fine." Her voice was icy.

"Fine what?" I asked.

"We'll go back."

"Really?"

"Artie!" Mrs. Burt called, and he came out of the bedroom where he'd been playing. "Get your stuff together. I'm taking you back."

"Back where?" Artie asked.

"Home. Except you don't have a home, do you? I'll take you back to my place and we'll call Social

Services. They'll find you somewhere to live."

Artie ran over and clung to her. "I want to stay with you, Mrs. Burt."

"I want to stay with you, too, believe me. But your brother won't let you."

"Mrs. Burt," I said, getting off the floor. "That's not true."

"It is." Her voice cracked and tears filled her glasses. "They won't ever let you stay with me."

"Will they send me to the Pennypackers?" Artie asked.

"They won't, Artie," I said. "I won't let them."

Mrs. Burt said, "They're not going to listen to a boy."

"We're going to find Mom," I told Artie.

Mrs. Burt snorted and Artie wailed that he didn't want to. It made me so mad that I started shouting at Mrs. Burt.

"You don't know anything about our mother! You never even met her! She made a mistake. Maybe she's in the middle of another one, I don't know. I was too scared to stay and find out. But she was trying to make a better life for us. She was back at school so she wouldn't be a dropout anymore. So she could get a good job. She wants to be a nursing assistant."

Mrs. Burt stared at me.

"And anyway," I went on, "she's our mother. She loves us and we love her!"

"I love Mrs. Burt!" cried Artie.

"You can love Mrs. Burt, too," I said. "You can love as many people as you want."

Mrs. Burt got up off her chair and stumped to her room.

"Pack your stuff," she said, just before she slammed the door.

I dragged Artie to the bedroom and took the pillowcases off the pillows. I stuffed some clothes for him in one and handed it to him to put his toys in. He made his fierce face, sucking in his lips.

"Artie, don't even think about a fit. We don't have time. Look."

I opened Mom's wallet and showed him her I.D.

As soon as he saw her picture, he began to wail.

"Mo-o-o-m! I want my mo-o-om! Where's my mo-o-om!"

I wished I'd thought of doing it before.

I let him hold the wallet and kiss her picture while I finished packing. Then I went and knocked on Mrs. Burt's door.

She didn't answer. I called through it that we were ready to go. When she didn't answer a second time, I opened it.

She was lying on the bed holding her chest. Her cap had fallen off. She looked so old on the white pillow with her white hair and her white, white face.

"Mrs. Burt?"

"He's crying for his mother," she gasped.

"Is something the matter?"

"He wants his mother," she said.

"Of course he does," I said. "Half the time he doesn't know what he's saying. He's just a little kid."

"I lost my little boy." She started panting so that it was hard to make out what she said next. "Bad mother," I heard.

"She's not!" I said.

"Me," Mrs. Burt moaned.

I knew then that something awful was happening to her. I called to Artie, who peeked in the door, clutching the wallet.

"I think Mrs. Burt is sick."

Artie ran over. "Do you need me to pat your back, Mrs. Burt?"

"Oh, you dear child," she whimpered. "Don't leave me. Please don't leave me."

"Artie is staying, Mrs. Burt. I'm going to get help."

WALKING TO TOWN would take too long if Mrs. Burt was having a heart attack. Even if her heart was only breaking, it would take too long. Standing by the highway and waiting for a murderer to drive by would probably take too long as well. So would building a raft.

I put on the Stanfields. Mrs. Burt had explained why they were such good underwear, because wool stays warm even when it's wet. I was probably going to get wet.

We actually hadn't swum in the lake since we swam across it. We didn't even wash in it anymore because it was too cold. Mrs. Burt heated water on the stove for us instead.

I grabbed my life jacket and the air mattress by the stove. Dressed only in socks and long underwear, I went down to the shore and put my hand in.

The lake bit me. The cold crunched right down on my bones and hurt so much I had to pull my hand back.

As I put on the life jacket, I looked across to where Mr. Munro's smoke was curling up. The trees on the far shore looked like they were all on fire. While I'd been lying by the stove in the cabin, they'd changed color. The earth had turned and turned all the way to autumn.

I slid the air mattress into the water and I threw myself on top of it, trying not to get wet. Pushing off, one foot dipped in the icy water. Then I had to paddle, plunge my arms in right up to my elbows. Pretty soon they were numb. I was moving forward so slowly it would be winter by the time I reached Mr. Munro's place, if I reached it alive.

I had no choice. I had to swim. Holding my breath, I slid off the side of the mattress into the cold. There was only one way to beat it. By moving.

I *can*, I told myself.

For a few minutes I swam without looking around. When I popped up, it seemed that I hadn't moved at all, that the smoke wasn't any closer.

"Blast it!" I said. "Blast it, blast it!"

Then I looked back and saw the air mattress floating far behind me.

But there was still a long way to go. When I swam with Mrs. Burt, it took twenty-four minutes to get across and thirty-three minutes to come back. Mr. Munro's place was closer than the far shore, but the water was so much colder, and the life jacket held me back.

I kept on muttering, "Blast it! Blast it!" I probably sounded crazy, thrashing and swearing.

Next time I looked up, I'd almost reached the bay where Mr. Munro's cabin was.

I made for the rocks and when I crawled up on them, I saw the four or five tumbledown cabins leaning into each other. I was shivering so badly I hardly had the strength to pull myself out of the water. I tried yelling, but my voice sounded so weak and old. There was no way Mr. Munro would hear me from inside.

Then I remembered the whole reason I was there. Because of Mrs. Burt. Mrs. Burt who was probably dying.

Because my hands wouldn't open or close, I pulled myself up with my forearms. Once I was standing, I couldn't take a single step. I just stood there, swaying and helpless.

Like Mrs. Burt. I felt like Mrs. Burt.

14

"You're a very brave young man," Marianne said.

"Not really," I said. "I was scared."

We were in her hotel room close to the hospital, waiting for Mom and Artie to get back from our old apartment. Marianne asked me to stay and tell her the whole story, and when I was finished, she offered to order me something from room service. I was hungry from all that talking.

She pushed the menu across to me. Like Mrs. Burt, feeding people seemed to make her happy. Other than that, she was so different. She wore makeup and nice clothes and her teeth were white and straight. You would never guess they were even related, let alone mother and daughter.

I asked for a grilled cheese sandwich and a glass of milk, and Marianne went over to the phone and ordered it. She came back and sat across from me again at the little table with the same sad expression she'd been wearing the whole time I was talking. Well, I'm not sure it was the whole time because, at different points in the story, she walked around the room, or stood with her back to me, staring out the window. Some of the things I said must have really hurt her feelings, especially the part where Mrs. Burt called her a Big Shot. I didn't want to repeat that, but Marianne asked me to tell her everything and be truthful.

"What about Mr. Munro?" she asked. "What did he say when you showed up?"

"He jumped out of his chair like a jack-in-the-box. I didn't knock, just sort of fell inside. He dragged me over to the stove and stripped the Stanfields off me. Then he forced some of the stuff from his flask down my throat because I was shivering so hard and crying that I was dying and so was Mrs. Burt. When he finally sorted it out, he called for help. He had a short-wave radio."

After I defrosted, Mr. Munro gave me some funny-smelling too-big clothes to put on and we set off in the canoe back to Mrs. Burt's place, with me huddled in a blanket in the bottom.

It seemed so quiet on the lake, like all the sounds had frozen except for Mr. Munro's paddle swishing through the water. When the droning started in the distance, I looked up. The first thing I thought was that it had been a while since I'd seen a dragonfly. Here came one now, the biggest ever, getting huger. Mr. Munro stopped paddling and both of us ducked as the plane sailed right over our heads and landed in the middle of the lake.

"It was a floatplane," I told Marianne.

I knew she hadn't been listening. It was the end of the story anyway, so I asked, "Is Mrs. Burt going to be okay?"

Marianne frowned. "She'll recover from the stroke. How did you find out about your mother?"

"The pilot told me. The paramedics brought Mrs. Burt out of the cabin on a stretcher and put her in the plane. When Artie and I got in, the pilot said, 'Looks like we found the two fellas everybody's been searching for.' He was the one who told us Mom was okay."

"It must have been a terrible shock."

"I guess, but I just started jabbing Artie and saying, 'See? See?' Because I *knew* she wouldn't take off again. I just *knew* it. She promised."

That last night we saw Mom, she got off the bus at her usual stop, three blocks from the gas station. She crossed the street near the stop like she did every night she worked at Pay-N-Save.

Except that night she never made it to the other side. Two cars were racing each other down the empty street but only one stopped. The other went through the red light and hit her. Both cars took off. When the ambulance got there, they found an unconscious woman in the road with no I.D. One leg was completely smashed. For almost two weeks she was in a coma.

When she finally woke up, the first thing she said was, "Where are my kids?"

Room service knocked and a waiter in a shirt and tie delivered my lunch on a tray. The milk was in a wine glass, the cloth napkin folded in a fan. There was a silver dome over the plate, which he lifted off, sort of bowing at the same time. Grilled cheese sandwich, French fries, coleslaw, a miniature pickle.

I ate the pickle. Then I offered Marianne some fries.

She shook her head. "Go ahead. Please. Eat."

She watched, but it didn't seem to make her happy. I felt self-conscious and wiped my mouth with the napkin. She must have realized she was staring because she picked up the book about King Arthur I'd brought and started leafing through it.

"Is it a good book?" she asked.

"Pretty good. I'm just reading about chivalry. I

thought the knights only had to slay monsters or find the Holy Grail, but they also had to swear to be kind and patient and have good manners. Stuff like that. They're like the rules Mr. Bryant gave us at the beginning of school last year. He was asking us to be knights, but I didn't know it."

She smiled and set the book beside the tray.

"How's the sandwich?"

"It's good," I told her. "But Mrs. Burt's are *way* better."

When I said that, Marianne started to cry.

"Sorry," I said.

"It's not your fault."

She went to the bathroom for a minute, then came back drying her eyes with a tissue.

"You must have been worried about your mother, too," I said. "Where did you think she'd gone?"

"Not to the cabin. She wouldn't ever go back after Clyde drowned. Of course, I never connected her to you and your brother, even though it was in the news. But afterward I remembered something. When my mother didn't answer the phone for a week, I flew out. I saw Artie's drawing on her fridge. The one of her with the walker and the rainbow shooting out the hose. I looked at it and thought, She doesn't know any kids. She doesn't even like kids. She doesn't like anybody."

"She loves Artie," I said. "And he loves her."

"Then there's another good deed you did without even knowing it," Marianne said. "Some people are so angry at themselves that they won't let anyone get close. It really says something about you and your brother that she let you love her."

"Artie. Not me. She mostly made me mad."

Marianne laughed, not a ha-ha laugh. A helpless one. Then she told me something really sad.

"She's a dropout, too, you know. She never finished high school. She ran off into the woods after my dad. He wouldn't have married her if she hadn't. That's how she ended up cooking in the camp. All those mean things she said about your mother? She was really saying them about herself."

That shocked me. I sat for a minute trying to believe it.

Artie and Mom came back soon after that. I jumped up to answer the door, grabbing Mom before she even stepped into the room.

Artie and I can't stop touching her now. We're afraid she'll get lost again if we don't hold onto her. If we don't touch her and smell her special lotion smell and play with her hair, which she got cut short when she was in the hospital. I can tell it sometimes hurts her to be pulled this way and that, like a stuffed toy we're fighting over, but she never complains. I think she's afraid of losing us again, too.

I helped her over to the chair. Artie held her other hand and dragged along the cane. As far as Artie is concerned, that cane — chrome just like the walker! — is the good thing that I promised would come out of all this. It's his horse and his sword and his magic wand. As soon as Mom's leg heals from this last operation, she'll walk fine and won't need it anymore.

Marianne put the room service tray in the hall and sat on the bed to watch us. Mom had the ring box, all mummied now with masking tape.

"Curtis?" she said. "I would never have thought to look there."

"Did they let you in the bedroom?"

"Yes, but they had a dresser standing right over the place."

She let Artie rip the tape off and lift the lid off the box. Then she took the note, unfolded and read it. She smiled and passed it to Marianne. While Marianne read it, Mom got Artie's tooth out of her wallet and put it in the ring box with mine. She snapped it closed. The sound was like everything clicking into place.

"Can I see it?" Marianne asked Artie. "The nice space where your tooth was."

He showed her, poking his pink tongue in and out of the hole.

The plan was that after Mom and Artie came back with the tooth, we were all going to visit Mrs. Burt. But Marianne wanted to talk to us first. She said sorry for about the thousandth time for what happened. Even though she was a lawyer, she wasn't getting involved. If the police pressed charges, they would be serious. Unlawful confinement, for one, she said.

Artie asked what that was. I told him it was sort of like kidnapping.

"Who did Mrs. Burt kidnap?" Artie asked.

Marianne didn't smile. "She kidnapped you and Curtis, Artie."

"She did not!"

"She asked us if we wanted to go," I said. "We said yes."

Then Marianne told us that Mrs. Burt hadn't been honest with us. She knew what had happened to Mom. The police told her the day she went over to our building. She took us away on false pretenses and she didn't take us back when I asked.

"Why wouldn't she tell us?" I asked.

Marianne sighed. "I don't know."

"Are you going to put her in a home?" Artie asked.

"She'll be lucky to go to a home. She could go to jail," Marianne said.

It took a moment for Artie to understand. When he did, he flung himself on the hotel floor, kicking and shrieking. Marianne drew back on the bed and stared at him, as though she'd never seen anything as horrible as a kid pitching a fit. After a minute, Mom reached for her cane and pressed the tip into Artie's stomach.

"That's enough," she said and, just like that, Artie stopped. It was like she pressed his Off button. He blinked up at her from the floor, then crawled into her lap and whimpered.

Mom turned to Marianne. "We really don't want charges laid. Look at my kids. They were probably better off than in foster care."

"It was fun!" Artie cried. "Except for the squirrels! We rode in three taxis and the Bel Air, and a *floatplane*! We got to pee outside!"

Marianne turned to me. "Curtis, you feel differently, don't you?"

Maybe I did, but now, after telling the whole story, so much of it seemed wonderful. Except for missing Mom, it was the best summer I ever had.

Besides, I didn't think she really meant to kidnap us.

"She was trying to help us," I said. "We were helping each other out."

❧

IN THE HOSPITAL, Artie dressed up as a knight with a towel from the hotel over his shoulders. But Mrs. Burt wouldn't see us. Marianne kept marching to the nursing station and demanding that they let her in. I would have hopped to it because she was pretty scary when she was acting like a lawyer.

The food cart was going around. Mom and Artie went to find a bathroom, and Marianne was trying to reach the doctor on her cellphone.

I told the man pushing the cart, "Tell the lady in Room 12 F that Artie wants to see her." If that didn't work, we might as well go home.

The man went in and came out. He asked, "Are you Curtis?"

"Yes."

"She says you can go in." I made him come over and tell it to the nurses so that I wouldn't get in trouble.

Mrs. Burt looked even worse than she had in

the cabin that last morning. Old and shrunk up in the bed, no cap, a needle taped in her arm.

"Hi," I said. "It's me, Sir Curtis."

Nothing.

"Mrs. Burt. I know you're not sleeping because your eyes are all scrunched up."

She opened them to glare at me. I smiled. Because if she was glaring, she must be getting better. But she still wouldn't talk. I wondered if she could. Mom said that sometimes you can't after a stroke.

So I started chattering like Artie. I told her Artie wanted to see her, and my mom wanted to thank her for taking care of us and feeding us. When I told her Marianne was there, too, Mrs. Burt scrunched her eyes up tighter and turned her head on the pillow.

"Why are you acting like this, Mrs. Burt? Marianne came all this way to see you."

Mrs. Burt turned her head straight on the pillow, but kept squinching.

"Why are you doing that with your eyes?" I asked.

Of course she could talk, I realized then. She'd told the food cart man to let me in. So I stopped talking, too. I just sat in the chair studying all the medical stuff in the room, the buttons and tubes and the plastic bag hanging from the pole that was dripping something into her arm.

Who would give up first? Me, probably. But I was wrong.

"I'm trying to die," Mrs. Burt said after a couple of minutes. Her voice sounded slurred and strange. She could only talk out of one side of her mouth. "I don't want to live anymore. I don't want to go to jail."

"You can't kill yourself with your eyes," I said.

"I'm using my will. I have a very strong will."

"I don't think you're going to jail, Mrs. Burt," I said.

"I am. I took you boys on purpose."

"Why didn't you tell us they'd found her?"

"They said she was all smashed up. She wouldn't have been able to look after you. Social Services would have got you anyway and I knew you didn't want to go with them."

"So you *were* trying to help us."

She grunted.

"That doesn't sound like kidnapping. That sounds like . . . absconding."

"No. Because I didn't give you the choice. I kept the truth from you. You gave me a postcard for your mother. I never mailed it."

Maybe I should have been mad when she told

me that, but I wasn't. Mom was back. Everything had worked out. Also, I felt sorry for her because she only waved one arm as she talked. The other lay on the bed like it was sleeping.

How would she manage when she got out of the hospital?

"What are you thinking?" she asked after a minute.

I was thinking that she would probably have to go into a home after all.

Unless.

Unless we helped her. I thought we could. Help her. But I didn't say it yet.

I smiled. "You should let Marianne come in."

"I can't!" she cried.

"Why not?"

The arm that could move reached for me, then dropped back on the bed like it was embarrassed.

"You were so good. Marianne was like that, too."

"Then why don't you tell her?"

Mrs. Burt clamped her eyes tight again.

I stood up.

"I'm going to let them in," I said. I didn't wait for her to answer.

Artie flew in the door in his cape the moment it opened, but stopped when he saw Mrs. Burt in the bed. She smiled at him from one side of her mouth. Then she looked up timidly at Mom and Marianne.

Marianne came over and took her hand. I think Mrs. Burt was going to say something, that she was sorry, maybe even that she loved her. I'm pretty sure, because it was written in all the lines on her face, except just then Artie rushed forward and offered to pat her back.

Mrs. Burt began to cry.

"Artie, my gas is gone. Ever since the stroke, it went. They say my arm will be able to move again if I do the therapy, but my gas might never come back."

We all laughed. We couldn't help it. Then Artie patted her back anyway.

She needed it.

She needed us.

Acknowledgments

A gargantuan thank-you to Shelley Tanaka for helping to make this novel a readable story and to Jackie Kaiser for finding it such a happy home. The inspiration for the lake in the middle of nowhere is Big Quarry Lake on Nelson Island, British Columbia. I am grateful to my generous in-laws, Joan and Graham Sweeney, for allowing us to holiday on Nelson Island every year. And, of course, nothing would be possible without Bruce and Patrick.

About the Author

Caroline Adderson is the author of several award-winning books for adults and children. Her works of adult fiction (*Bad Imaginings*, *A History of Forgetting*, *Sitting Practice, Pleased to Meet You* and *The Sky Is Falling*) have been nominated for the Governor General's Award, the Rogers Writers' Trust Fiction Prize, the Giller Prize and the Commonwealth Writers' Prize. She is a three-time CBC Literary Award winner, two-time winner of the Ethel Wilson Fiction Prize and recipient of the 2006 Marian Engel Award for her body of work.

Caroline's children's books include *I, Bruno* (nominated for the Chocolate Lily and Shining Willow book awards), *Very Serious Children* (winner of the Diamond Willow Award and shortlisted for the Rocky Mountain Book Award) and the Jasper John Dooley series.

She lives in Vancouver with her husband and son.